A crack of gunfire reverberated from the trees.

"Get inside," Chris shouted.

Lauren was already running. The door was two-inch-thick solid oak with a steel core. Lauren slammed it and threw the two dead bolts into place.

She flung herself to the floor. "Who's shooting at us?"

"Maybe you tell me." Chris sank onto the edge of the leather sofa. "Your brother?"

"But−" Lauren leaned against the breakfast bar, her heart racing. "That wasn't you shooting at Ryan?"

"I never saw Ryan."

She swallowed. "He took off when the shooting started."

Chris gazed at her with narrowed eyes, then glanced toward the steps to the bedrooms above, and back to her. "You know, if you harbor a fugitive, you're an accessory−"

"He isn't here." Lauren flung her arms wide. "Go look for yourself, if you don't believe me. I should have known you'd come here. Your first thought was that Lauren would protect her brother." She blinked hard against hot moisture in her eyes.

"You've always put your brother first."

Laurie Alice Eakes dreamed of being a writer from the time she was a small child. Now, with her dreams fulfilled, she is the award-winning and bestselling author of over two dozen historical and contemporary novels. When she isn't writing full-time, she enjoys long walks, live theater and being near her beloved Lake Michigan. She lives in Illinois with her husband and sundry cats and dogs.

Books by Laurie Alice Eakes

Love Inspired Suspense

Perilous Christmas Reunion

PERILOUS CHRISTMAS REUNION

LAURIE ALICE EAKES

HARLEQUIN® LOVE INSPIRED® SUSPENSE

Recycling programs
for this product may
not exist in your area.

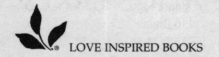

LOVE INSPIRED BOOKS

ISBN-13: 978-1-335-49081-0

Perilous Christmas Reunion

www.Harlequin.com

Printed in U.S.A.

But I say unto you which hear, Love your enemies, do good to them which hate you, Bless them that curse you, and pray for them which despitefully use you. And unto him that smiteth thee on the one cheek offer also the other; and him that taketh away thy cloak forbid not to take thy coat also. Give to every man that asketh of thee; and of him that taketh away thy goods ask them not again. And as ye would that men should do to you, do ye also to them likewise. For if ye love them which love you, what thank have ye? for sinners also love those that love them. And if ye do good to them which do good to you, what thank have ye? for sinners also do even the same. And if ye lend to them of whom ye hope to receive, what thank have ye? for sinners also lend to sinners, to receive as much again. But love ye your enemies, and do good, and lend, hoping for nothing again; and your reward shall be great, and ye shall be the children of the Highest: for he is kind unto the unthankful and to the evil. Be ye therefore merciful, as your Father also is merciful.

–Luke 6:27-36

For Sandra Robbins: Without your generosity of time and patience, this book never would have happened.

ONE

Lauren Wexler spied the man the instant he stepped from beneath the shadowing tree branches and into the clearing. Moonlight reflecting off snow lit him like a stage spotlight, highlighting the chiseled bones of his face and dark hollows of his eyes, his long form more skinny than lean.

Heart thudding hard enough to make her sick to her stomach, Lauren left the picture window and flung open the door. A gust of wind seized it from her hand, sending it slamming back against its stopper and flames hissing and roaring in the stove. Knowing the gusts from the coming storm would snatch away her words, she stepped onto the deck and cupped her hands around her mouth. "Ryan Delaney, I told you not to come here."

"Lauren, you've got to help me." He started racing toward her, his footfalls crunching through the ice-topped snow. "Please."

"I can't." She stepped over the threshold and reached for the door handle.

Ryan might be her older brother, but he was also a wanted man.

"You need to turn yourself in." She started to close the door.

Ryan had nearly reached the deck. "But, Lauren, they're going to—"

A shot rang out from the nearby trees, and Ryan landed on the deck's bottom step, hand scrabbling at the ice-coated wood.

"Ryan!"

Wounded or making himself a lower profile for the shooter?

"Ryan?" She called his name again.

"Help me." He tried hauling himself up the treads, but slipped back to the piled snow at the foot of the steps. "Help me."

He must be wounded. She couldn't leave him there in the cold, in danger. But she could get shot herself if she went to him.

Criminal or not, he was her brother, her half brother to be precise, and needed help.

Crouching below the deck rails to make herself a more difficult target, she crawled to the steps. Lying flat, she reached down the steps to grasp Ryan's hand. "Can you crawl up the steps? I can—"

Another gun blast reverberated over the frozen lake and leafless trees. This time, she heard the buzz of a bullet not far enough over her head for comfort. Her heart stuttered.

Ryan grasped her wrist. "Go back inside before they…hurt you."

"Who?"

"Get inside…now." Ryan squeezed her hand, then scrambled to his feet and pounded across the lakeshore to the woods on the other side of the clearing. Even the clouds beginning to obscure the moonlight could not blot out the dark stain on the snow where Ryan had lain, nor the patches left in his wake.

He was injured and running for his life, leading the shooter away from her.

After he'd pressed something small and hard into her hand.

She shoved the plastic rectangle into her pocket and stared after her brother's retreating form. She wanted to follow, to bind up his wound. She knew locking herself in the house made more sense. Sending away a fugitive brother was one thing. Sending away a wounded fugitive brother without offering aid first was quite another.

Two more shots in rapid succession decided her action. She started to rise enough to creep back into the house.

"Freeze! Deputy US Marshal." The voice rang through the night, shooting into Lauren's heart like one of the flying bullets.

Deputy US Marshal. Of course, they were hunting Ryan. Thousands of marshals existed. He could be any of them. It didn't have to be *him*.

Heart racing, Lauren charged toward the still-open door. Bullets whizzed past her head. One slammed into the doorjamb, the other soared into the house's interior. Lauren dived for the floor of the deck and rolled behind the woodpile.

More gunfire exploded.

This time not from the trees.

A whimper escaping her lips despite her best efforts, Lauren curled into a fetal position behind the cords of wood stacked at the end of the deck. She shivered so hard from cold and fright she feared her chattering teeth would chip. If someone didn't shoot her, she was going to die from exposure. If only she had stayed in the house, closed the shutters, pretended she hadn't seen her brother racing across the lakeshore...

"Drop your weapons." Nearby, the authoritative voice cracked like breaking icicles—cold, sharp, familiar.

Silence fell. Lauren uncurled enough to peek around the end of the woodpile. She saw nothing but the trampled and stained snow where Ryan had run. She heard nothing but wind in the trees and the creak and crack of ice on the lake. Perhaps danger had moved on and she could return to the warmth of her house. Unable to feel anything but the warning tingle in her face, fingers and toes, Lauren crawled from behind the piled wood and started to rise.

Gunfire and shouts erupted across the clearing, one from the far side where Ryan had vanished, the other close at hand. Too close.

Before her shocked senses reacted, strong hands grasped her arms and dragged her back behind the woodpile. More gunfire. Louder. Closer. The man holding her grunted. One of his hands released. The other held tight, compelling her down, down, against the snow-coated wood. The logs rumbled and began to roll.

Lauren wrenched herself to one side, avoiding the avalanche. The man holding her wasn't so fortunate. He landed hard, a deadweight with wood piling atop him.

A deadweight.

Lauren prayed he hadn't been shot or killed, not for her sake. He'd had to rescue her because she was out trying to save her brother. If she hadn't gone after Ryan, this wouldn't have happened. Whether marshal or miscreant, she must help this man who had probably saved her life.

Conscious she was an easy next target, Lauren began to toss logs aside to get to the man beneath. He was going to be crushed. He was going to die. He might have been dead before the wood cascaded upon him. He had fallen against the cords of fuel immediately after the last gunfire.

Anxiety over the horror she might encounter didn't stop her. In the event he still breathed, she couldn't leave him there. She couldn't take the time to call for help. Once she knew one way or the other, she would contact the emergency responders.

"Don't let him be dead. Please, God, don't let this man be dead."

Removing another log, she saw he wasn't crushed at all. Logs had tumbled in a pyramid over him, forming a hollow beneath. But he was injured. Blood marred the pristine snow, just as she'd feared. He had been shot.

The last of the wood sailed out of her hands and landed with a *kerchunk* atop its fellow sawed logs. Lauren got her first sight of the prone man from head to toe. He was tall and athletic, the latter obvious even through his bulky winter clothing. A rip in that clothing showed Lauren where the bullet had struck, yet no blood seeped from the hole. Instead, it matted his short dark hair.

For a moment, she stared at the hole in his coat. Then she touched it. No, the fabric was not absorbing any liquid. The wound was dry.

His head was another matter. If he'd been shot in the head, his situation could be dire. She needed to look, discover the extent and cause of the damage.

Not that she was much of a medic. Her skills lay in software engineering, not skull fractures.

Before inspecting the fallen man's head wound more

closely, Lauren checked for a pulse. Beneath his down coat, his skin was warm, his neck a little rough with a day's growth of whiskers. But his pulse was strong. He was only unconscious.

And likely smothering in the snow. Somehow, she had to get him up and out of the frosty night before he died of hypothermia.

"Before *we* die of hypothermia." Lauren spoke between teeth clenched to stop their chattering. "Sir, can you hear me? Sir?" She shook his shoulder.

He groaned.

"Sir, I need you to wake up and get into the house. I'm not strong enough to carry you."

She was a small woman, and he was nearly twice her size.

"I can help you."

Briefly, she recalled something about not moving someone with a head injury in the event their spine was involved. Moving the victim could cause more damage. Yet staying out in the cold would definitely cause damage—permanent damage, like death. Given the choice, she decided to do what she could to move him.

She curved one hand around the back of his neck and gripped his uninjured shoulder with the other to roll him onto his side. He groaned again and strong fingers inside leather gloves gripped her wrist.

"The other way." He spoke in a raspy murmur, yet the voice was familiar—that authoritative ring, that masculine timbre.

Her heart squeezed at the idea of who this might be chasing down her brother, saving her from gunmen, making breathing difficult and speaking even harder.

"You have a hole there. I didn't want to grab the shoulder where you were shot and cause more harm."

"Kevlar vest." He took a deep breath and moaned.

Despite the softness of his words, she knew for certain who had saved her from a gunshot wound. Christopher Blackwell, the man she'd never expected to come near her again after how she'd treated him. And she was sure he wouldn't have if her brother were not a fugitive and Chris weren't a deputy US marshal.

If Chris weren't a deputy US marshal, they would be married, not estranged.

As though nothing unpleasant had ever lain between them, he continued to speak. "Bullet didn't go through, but hurts like…crazy. And my head…" He raised one hand toward his temple.

Lauren caught his wrist. "Don't. You're bleeding. You'll ruin your gloves."

She could play this we're-just-strangers-caught-in-a-weird-situation-together game as well as he could.

"And I'm going to need them."

He was right about that. Wind gusted off the lake, and clouds thickened across the moon.

The chattering of Lauren's teeth increased too much to disguise, and she wished blood wasn't smeared over her hands so she could free her hair from its nighttime braid to serve as a sort of cloak for her ears and shoulders.

"We c-can't stay out-t here any l-longer." She shuddered with the next blast of damp wind. "How can I best get you up?"

"Can you get one arm beneath me? You're just a little thing, but even a bit of a boost should help get me going in the right direction."

He had always referred to her as being "a little thing." The memory stabbed her like an icicle to the heart. Slipping her arm around him, feeling the power of his body, the heat through his coat, would be like an entire eave's worth of icicles piercing the wall of her chest—the barricade she'd erected around her emotions.

But her exposed skin had long ago begun to tingle, and if she didn't want frostbite, she needed to get him up and into the house.

"Okay, ready?" Her face turned toward the woods, where the branches had begun to lash the darkening sky, Lauren slipped one arm beneath Chris's shoulders. Her hand touched cold snow and colder metal, as she curled her fingers around the bulky muscle of his upper arm. Not until she heaved with all her strength did she realize the metal must belong to his gun. It had either slipped from his holster when he fell, or he had been holding it, ready to fire. Or…

She jerked her hand away. "Did you shoot my brother?"

Chris started to sigh in exasperation. Pain shot through his back, bruised, no doubt, from the bullet that had slammed into his vest, so he settled for a quick puff through his clenched teeth. "I did not shoot your brother. It's quite likely the other way around."

"Ryan would never shoot at either of us. Besides, he has never carried a gun." Lauren spoke with the harsh defense of her brother she always had, though she knew he operated outside the law more often than not.

The same sort of defense that had driven a tractor trailer–sized wedge between Chris and Lauren five years ago.

Remembered anguish roughened Chris's tone when he responded. "He stole one from the courtroom deputy today."

"But that—"

"Save it, Lauren. Someone has been out here shooting, and they may be circling around for a better shot."

"Someone shot Ryan." She scrambled to her feet. "He fell. He was bleeding."

If he was wounded, Chris had a better chance of capturing him. Maybe Ryan would be back in custody by no later than tomorrow, Christmas Eve, and no one else would have to sacrifice their holiday to continue the pursuit.

"Your head is bleeding pretty badly yourself." Lauren's tone softened. "Do you still need me to help you up?"

"No, ma'am." Chris grabbed a stick of kindling from the disordered cords of wood and used it as a crutch to haul himself to his feet. He swayed, feeling as though each gust of wind from the oncoming storm could blow him over.

Lauren touched his arm. "Let me help you inside before you fall down."

"I'm all right." He didn't look at her. He couldn't bring himself to read anger or disgust with his work in her beautiful face.

"Sure, you're all right. You always wobble when you're standing still." Her tone dripped with sarcasm, though she wrapped her arm around his waist. "Put your arm around my shoulders and we'll get into the house before we turn into snowpeople…or get shot."

"If I fall again, I'll drag you down with me."

He regretted the words the instant he said them. They

were too much of a reminder of her words when she broke their engagement.

With the way people think, if my family falls, my credibility may go down with them, regardless of how innocent I am. And I would drag your career as a marshal with me.

"I'm sorry." Chris slung an arm over her shoulders more as an apology than because he needed her physical support.

She said nothing. Head bowed, she trekked through the snow more slowly than he liked with at least one gunman possibly still lurking in the trees biding his time for—what? A better shot at the deputy marshal, if it was Ryan who had done the firing? For Ryan to reappear, if this was a separate gunman? Chris hadn't seen Ryan, or anyone other than Lauren. He had seen only the muzzle flashes, heard the shots echoing from the trees and across the frozen lake.

Chris fought the urge to run. He wasn't sure he could, and Lauren wore ridiculous slipper things on her feet that would probably make her fall at a faster gait. They didn't have far to go along the length of the deck. Their footfalls made nearly no sound in the powdered snow blown across the boards. In contrast, the wind through the bare tree branches sounded like torrential rain. Ice along the shoreline cracked with the onslaught of rising waves. Although the first flakes of snow heralded the coming storm, Lauren no longer shivered. Chris understood why—maybe. Lauren's nearness warmed him, and she might feel the same, despite the coldness that had frozen communication between them when he'd changed career paths.

The fifteen feet to the door felt like fifteen miles.

So close to Lauren, Chris caught her scent, sweet and delicate like orange blossoms. He tried not to breathe. He tried not to remember how being near her had once made him feel.

They reached the house. Through the open door, heat from the wood-burning stove poured over them like hot syrup, along with the fragrance of bacon and fresh bread and sugar cookies.

"I'll just grab my first-aid kit." She called out her intent without looking back, then raced for the bathroom.

Chris closed and bolted the door, then headed for the stove with its radiating heat. It needed another log to really be effective. With a gunman probably still outside somewhere, he should close her shutters and—

He clapped his hand to his side. His gun. It wasn't in its holster. He had removed it to fire back at the rifleman in the trees long enough for Lauren to get to safety. Riflemen in the trees. More than one shooter. He had made the rookie mistake of thinking all he heard behind him were echoes. Apparently another man had been behind him, shooting him in the back, and he had fallen, logs burying him and crashing into his head so hard he feared he lost consciousness for a minute or two. He must have dropped the gun when he fell.

Cautious, all too aware the fugitive was likely still armed from his daring escape from the courtroom that morning, Chris opened the door. Wind threatened to snatch it from his hand. He muscled the door shut behind him and paused to listen.

If anyone still lurked in the trees, the wind masked any sound they made. Scudding clouds and waving branches disguised anything else moving in the shadows. But he dared not leave his weapon in the snow. He might want it. Judging from how the night was going, he would need it.

Still dizzy from the blow to his head, his upper back throbbing with every breath, Chris braced one hand against the side of the house to traverse the fifteen feet to the woodpile at the end of the deck. He was partially sheltered there by the house and the stacked cordwood. No one raced along the lakeshore or across the frozen water. But those trees could hold any kind of menace.

He dropped to a crouch and began to hunt for his weapon amid the disordered logs. Nothing. No glint of waning moonlight on steel. No unmistakable dark shape against the snow. The place where he had fallen was clear of wood. Blood from his head wound was a dark stain against the white. Yet no gun lay amid the wreckage.

He guessed what had happened to it. Lauren had stopped while investigating his injuries and accused him of shooting her brother, most likely because she had found his weapon.

"Chris?" Lauren called from the doorway.

"Stop." He turned and held up his hand, palm toward her.

She stopped on the threshold. "Do you need my help?"

"I need your help all right." His insides as cold as the lake, Chris stalked toward the door. "You can help by telling me what you did with my gun."

Lauren stared at him. "What are you talking about?"

"My gun." He gestured toward the ground where he'd been lying. "My weapon. It isn't here."

TWO

Lauren crossed her arms over her chest and grasped her elbows to stop herself from shaking—from cold or in response to the fury on Chris's face, she wasn't quite sure. "I know your gun was there. I felt it when I was helping you get up, but I didn't take it."

Chris pressed one hand to his head, where blood still trickled along his hairline, then bent to roll aside a log at the same moment a crack of gunfire reverberated from the trees.

"Get inside," Chris shouted.

Lauren was already running for the open door. Chris caught up and grabbed her hand. Her moccasins slipped on the doorsill, and she landed on her knees. Chris edged past her, then bent to catch hold of her arms and haul her to her feet. A sharp hiss of breath through his teeth reminded Lauren he was injured, and she freed herself from his grip so she could slip her arm around his waist and propel him through the door.

It was two-inch-thick, oak with a steel core, meant to withstand a Michigan winter or the worst summer storm. Lauren slammed it and threw the two dead bolts into place. The storm shutters were already closed, save for the one over the front window. Chris lunged for that one and banged it shut. A moment later, another shot cracked, muffled by the cabin's thick walls, but the walls weren't so thick Lauren missed the thud of a bullet striking the window frame.

"What are they doing?" She flung herself to the floor below the level of the window. "Who is shooting at us?"

"Maybe you can tell me." Pallor emphasizing the deep blue of his eyes, Chris sank onto the edge of the leather sofa. "Your brother?"

"But—" Lauren stood and leaned against the wall, her heart racing as though she had just finished swimming across the lake "—that wasn't you shooting at Ryan?"

"I never saw Ryan. Where did he go?"

"He took off when the shooting started."

Chris gazed at her with narrowed eyes, then glanced toward the steps to the bedrooms above and back to her. "You know, if you harbor a fugitive, you're an accessory—"

"He isn't here." Lauren flung her arms wide, nearly knocking a poinsettia off a low table. "Go look for yourself, if you don't believe me. I know that's why you're here. I should have known you'd come here first."

"I was on my way to see my family when the news hit."

"And your first thought was that Lauren would protect her brother." She blinked hard against hot moisture in her eyes.

"You've always put your brother first."

She spun on her heel, numb with cold from her wet moccasins, and stalked into the kitchen. "I never put Ryan first, but you will never understand that I can't stop loving him just because he might associate with criminals."

"'Might associate with'?" Chris's voice was far too quiet.

Lauren understood what that meant. He grew quiet when he was angry. She supposed she couldn't blame him. Her family had come between Chris and her having a happy future together. Now Ryan was interfering with Chris's Christmas with his mother and sister.

And she had just said that Ryan might associate with criminals, as though he wasn't one himself. She never could accept that her big brother was something other than the kind and loving young man who had built her a tree house and cleaned her bloody hands and knees when she was learning to ride a bike.

"Ryan ran into the woods when the shooting started." As an olive branch, her information was poor, but it was all she had to offer.

"Do you have any form of communication here?" Chris's question was his only response. "I get no signal on my mobile."

Despite the heavy storm shutters, she was all too aware of a gunman likely lurking outside the house. Without a word, she fetched the satellite phone and handed it to Chris, then she located the first-aid kit she had dropped on the faded Oriental rug in the center of the living room. She could doctor Chris's head wound until he got assistance from EMTs. Needing warm water to cleanse the wound, she returned to the kitchen. With the open floor plan, she wouldn't be able to avoid hearing Chris's call, but if he wanted privacy, he could go into the bathroom, one of the bedrooms or even retreat upstairs.

Yet he made no phone calls. One hand holding a square of clean linen cloth beneath the kitchen tap, Lauren glanced over her shoulder. Chris perched on the edge of the sofa with the phone in his hand, his mouth set in a grim line.

"What's wrong?" She flicked off the water.

"No signal. I guess I have to risk going outside."

"You shouldn't have to. I have an antenna." Their eyes met across the breakfast bar, and she corrected herself. "I had an antenna."

"Cloud interference?"

"The weather isn't bad enough for that yet." Despite the heat of the woodstove, a chill raced down Lauren's arms. When she read the accusation in Chris's gaze, steady upon her face, the shivers penetrated through her body to her core. She would rather face an arctic storm outside than remain beneath the scrutiny of those beautiful blue eyes. Yet she could not look away or he would think she was trying to hide something.

"Did you disable the antenna because you were expecting your brother?" He asked the question she had anticipated.

She flattened the palms of her hands on the white quartz countertop so they wouldn't shake. "Do you really think I climbed on the roof to disable the antenna?"

"I think you didn't answer my question." His tone was as cold as Lauren felt—a rival to the oncoming storm—cold enough to make something inside her snap.

"I did not disable the antenna." She threw the cloth she'd been wetting into the sink. "I did not plan to give my brother shelter." She grabbed the frying pan with her ruined dinner congealing inside and threw that into the sink with a satisfying clatter of cast iron on stainless steel. "I did not shoot at you, steal your gun or make the woodpile collapse on top of you. I arrived here two hours ago to avoid the press that seems to be forgetting it is nearly Christmas and some of us would like a peaceful time to remember the season and the birth of Jesus in peace. I came here to avoid the press so I didn't forget about goodwill toward men." She rounded the breakfast bar and yanked open the door to the stove to add more wood. "I was not in Chicago for my brother's trial, so I did not aid and abet his escape." A log slipped from her hands and hit the floor a hairbreadth from her toes. "I cannot prove the negative, so you will simply have to believe me or not. Frankly, at this moment, goodwill toward men does not include you, as far as I'm concerned." She wrestled the log into the stove and latched the door before she dared face a too-silent and, she presumed, outraged deputy US marshal.

She faced a man with one arm clamped to his side and his other hand flattened to the wound on his head, as he rocked with silent laughter.

"I'm glad I amuse you." Burdened with the knowledge she had just made a fool of herself, she trudged back to the kitchen and found another clean cloth. "Your head is bleeding again. Let me clean it up and get a bandage on it." The running water masked anything he might have said. By the time the cloth was wet and she returned to the living room, Chris had stopped laughing. The light had left his eyes, and his jaw, solid and square, was set in renewed anger, or maybe just pain— set enough so he didn't seem inclined to speak.

Lauren took a deep breath. "I apologize for losing my temper. I simply—" She broke off, not willing to diminish the apology with excuses about how much she hated false accusations. "Please forgive me. My temper is my thorn in my flesh."

"I know." Their eyes met again. From only two feet away, the impact struck Lauren like a physical blow to her chest, to her heart.

He had always laughed at her temper, those infrequent outbursts after she was pushed too far. At least he had laughed until the last time when she had sent him away in a flood of outrage, a spate of words designed to drown any affection he felt for her.

She held up the wet cloth like a shield. "Let me cleanse that wound for you. Do you think it was from a bullet too?"

"A log struck me. I doubt I'd be awake if it had been a gunshot wound."

"I suppose not." She brushed aside his hair, cut short no doubt for his job, but so thick it tended to wave anyway, so dark a brown it was nearly black, far darker than her own burnished chestnut. "It's not deep. I don't think you'll need stitches."

"That's fortunate, since we can't seem to get an ambulance or sheriff here." He held up the useless sat phone.

"I could have stitched it."

"Without anesthesia? No thanks." He shuddered.

"You mean the big bad deputy marshal can't take a little pain?" She meant the words to be teasing; they sounded snarky.

In truth, they were mean. He must be in serious pain from the blow to his back, vest or not, but hadn't complained about it. His head must hurt, as well. Again, he hadn't complained.

"I'm sorry," she said.

"No need to apologize for that."

"Which means I need to apologize for something else." She affixed a couple of butterfly bandages to the wound, covered them with a larger adhesive-edged pad and stepped back to inspect her work. "It'll do."

"Thank you." He gave her a half smile. "Now that I'm patched up, let's go back to talking about your brother."

She stiffened. "I do not need to apologize for helping my brother. I did nothing but go to him when he fell at the bottom of the steps, to offer him aid if he was seriously injured. He wasn't hurt that badly, apparently."

"That's all?" Chris's gaze burned into hers.

"Yes, that's—" Her hand dropped to the pocket of her jeans.

In all the terror of being shot at, not to mention the shock of seeing Chris after five years, she had forgotten about the flash drive Ryan had pressed into her hand.

Lauren paled, emphasizing the depths of her wide, dark eyes. Chris regretted his harshness, yet she needed to see the consequences of helping her brother evade the law. He might not be able to love a woman who could not support his chosen profession, but he remembered enough of his former affection for her to want to keep her free to live her life as she wished to.

"What is it?" Chris demanded.

"I...don't know. Maybe nothing." She pulled something from her pocket and held it out to him.

The dull black plastic of a flash drive lay stark against her pale skin.

"What is it?" Chris repeated.

"Ryan gave it to me before he got up and started running again, right before the shooting."

"And when were you going to tell me?"

"As soon as I remembered it."

Chris arched one brow in skeptical inquiry.

"I was a little distracted over being shot at." She spoke through gritted teeth. "I have no idea what's on it. I have no idea why he gave it to me, but you probably have more use for it than I do."

"I probably do." Chris started to reach for it, thought of fingerprints and snatched a piece of gauze from the first-aid kit.

"It already has my fingerprints on it, and Ryan was wearing gloves," Lauren pointed out.

"I don't need to add my fingerprints to what might be there." Chris wrapped the flash drive in gauze and slipped it into his pocket.

"Should I get my computer so you can see what's on it?" Lauren asked.

Chris studied her face for a moment, trying to look beyond the distraction of her beauty to discover if she was being sincerely cooperative or playing some kind of game. He couldn't forget his missing service weapon, nor the fact that Ryan had come straight to her, as Chris had suspected he would. He couldn't forget that Lauren had put her criminal family before him five years earlier.

With her final words—*I love you too much to let my family drag down your new career, but I can't give up the only family I have*—ringing in his ears, Chris made a decision.

"I'd rather give it to the nearest US marshal's office to look at."

"Even if it holds a key to where Ryan has gone?"

"Good point, but I can wait until I get my own laptop out of my SUV. It's parked along the highway."

Lauren gave him an exasperated glance. "My computer is about five feet from you. You're welcome to use it."

And have some special encryption erase the drive the instant he inserted it?

"You." She flung up her hands. "Do you think I'll destroy the data on that thing by some technical sleight of hand?"

"You are a computer whiz, aren't you? The successful computer-security entrepreneur?"

"I am," she said without conceit, "and I am also a law-abiding citizen with some compassion. Since you're hungry, I can make us some dinner."

Chris's eyes widened. "You read minds?"

"I hear growling stomachs—yours and mine. Come sit at the breakfast bar while I cook."

Chris tried to rise. Pain shot through his back, and a groan slipped from his lips before he could suppress it.

"You need a doctor." Lauren grasped his upper arm on the unwounded side. "Let me help." She tugged.

With her help and some gritting of his teeth, he managed to get his legs beneath him enough to fight the softness of the sofa and stand. "I don't need medical help, but we do need to get that flash drive to law enforcement tonight. If you have any ideas how we will do that, you have better resources than I do."

As if to emphasize his words, a gust of wind howled around the corner of the house, and icy pellets chattered against the windows.

"There's a Jeep and a snowmobile in the garage."

Lauren gathered up her first-aid kit and headed to the kitchen.

"Of course you have a four-wheel drive vehicle and a snowmobile." Relief filled Chris as he perched on one of the stools at the breakfast bar. "Either would work if we knew someone wasn't out there taking potshots at us."

"'Someone'? You mean my brother."

"I mean someone after your brother—or you."

"Me?" About to pick up the frying pan from the sink, she spun to face him.

"You made contact with Ryan. Ryan was about to accept a plea bargain in court when he chose to run instead." Chris took in Lauren's blank look and wondered if being CEO of her own company had turned her into an excellent actress or if she truly didn't understand. He explained, "Ryan has information the government wants, information that can bring down a whole lot of bad guys. They want to stop him from talking. He thinks his life is threatened. If others believe Ryan told you something, your life is in danger, as well."

"I see." Lauren folded, held upright with her elbows on the breakfast bar and her face in her hands.

Once upon a time, Chris would have rounded the counter and offered her comfort. Now he sat gazing at her, tongue-tied, mind spinning to find something to tell her. All he seized upon was "I'll do my best to protect you."

Except his weapon was gone, possibly taken by her because Ryan had warned her of danger.

"You've already got hurt pushing me out of the way of a bullet." Her voice was muffled by her hands.

"Maybe my presence alone will be a deterrent. Injuring a deputy US marshal is asking for more attention and trouble than these guys want."

"That's good, with you hurt and all."

"I'm all right. Breathing hurts, but isn't excruciating. I think that's a good sign. If I may use one of your guest rooms until the weather improves..." He trailed off, not sure how to ask for something that made him seem like he was welcome.

"You can use either room upstairs." She turned her back on him and began to scrub the frying pan. "You'll probably find some of Ryan's clothes in the one at the top of the steps. They're old, but they won't have holes in them."

"Thanks."

Wearing the clothes, even castoffs, of a man he was pursuing seemed vaguely unethical. But not taking advantage of dry clothes would be foolish.

He climbed the steps running along one wall of the living room and entered the bedroom at the top. It didn't look recently lived in. The bed was neatly made, the shutters closed, the curtains drawn. Though someone had cleaned away dust, the room smelled closed. Not musty, but stale. Were this a normal visit, Chris would have flung open the windows despite the cold and inhaled the glorious freshness of pine trees and the tang of wood smoke. But he didn't dare so much as look at the lake or glance to see how badly the snow was falling. Instead, he opened the door to the en suite bathroom and removed his many layers so he could examine the damage to his back with the aid of the mirror. Getting Lauren to look would be easier than twisting around, but no way would he ask that of her. It wasn't appropriate.

It wasn't necessary. He had a terrible bruise. Ice would benefit him.

Goose bumps rose on his skin at the idea of an ice pack. The fire's heat didn't reach the upper floor, and Lauren must have the propane furnace turned low to conserve fuel.

He found T-shirts and flannel button-downs in the dresser. They fitted a little too well. The jeans in another drawer proved too short, so he settled for a pair of sweatpants to get out of his own soaked trousers. He drew the line at wearing another man's socks, but he located a pair of fleece-lined moccasins in the closet. He shoved his cell phone and wallet with his deputy US marshal credentials into the pockets of the sweatpants, then glanced around for anything else he might need if he and Lauren had to evacuate the house in a hurry.

His boots. With the snow, he would need boots. In their wet state, however, they might take too long to pull on. His good snow boots were in his Jeep. He hadn't taken the time to change into them. He'd been too anxious to see if Ryan had gone to his sister.

He'd been too apprehensive about seeing Lauren again to remember his dress boots weren't effective in more than an inch or two of snow.

Back downstairs, Lauren stood at the stove, turning bacon in a pan. "I have frozen waffles and eggs, if you want those. Or bread for a sandwich. I was going to make BLTs before the shooting started."

"That sounds good." Chris hesitated in the opening to the kitchen. "Can I toast the bread or something?"

"Thanks. And slice the tomatoes?"

"Sure."

They worked in silence punctuated by the sizzle of bacon in the pan and the howl of the wind outside. A log shifted in the stove, the toaster sprang with golden-brown slices and still they said nothing. Lauren took the toast and tomatoes from Chris and piled on bacon and lettuce. Still neither of them spoke.

Then Lauren opened the refrigerator. "What do you want to drink? I have three kinds of pop, milk and orange juice."

"Can I trouble you for coffee?" Chris carried the plates of sandwiches to the small round table by the stove. "I need to warm up and stay awake."

"For what?" She began to run the coffee carafe beneath the tap. "You look like you need sleep."

He shouldn't care that she noticed his fatigue.

"I presume Ryan has a key to this house?"

"He does not." She set the carafe on the hot plate.

Chris watched her graceful movements, the sureness of each scoop and pour without scattering grounds across the countertop as he always did. She was smart and good at just about everything she tried—except for loving him.

He shook his head. "You expect me to believe you never gave a key to your big brother?"

"I expect you to believe the truth." She turned from the counter and filled two glasses with water. "Let's eat while it's warm."

They settled at the table, thick sandwiches and a bowl of apples between them. The table was so small their knees nearly touched. It was a table meant for playing board games. The dining table was across the room, in the shadows away from the warmth of the fire. That warmth eddied around them like an invisible cocoon holding them in the same place—a place full of memories of other meals shared at a similar table, of rainy days spent playing Scrabble or Monopoly at his mother's house.

If he hadn't needed fuel, Chris might have pushed away and retreated to the room upstairs. He didn't need reminders of that blissful summer in another cabin at another lake, before his father had died and he changed careers.

The crunching of teeth on toast and crisp bacon sounded like an army tramping over crusty snow.

Last week's warmer weather had given the snow an icy surface, a natural warning if anyone approached the cabin.

The howling wind and occasional rattle of a snapping tree branch suggested no one in his right mind would prowl outside. Getting inside wouldn't be easy without a key to the many locks on the doors.

Not easy, nor impossible.

"Why is this house built like a fortress?" Chris asked.

Those locks, heavy doors and solid shutters raised his law-enforcement antenna.

Lauren shrugged as though every house was built with so many reinforcements. "It wasn't built like a fortress. I had the doors changed to steel-cored and the shutters installed after those murderers escaped in New York and broke into summer cabins. I don't want anyone trashing this place when I'm not here, and I want to feel safe when I am."

"It's a good place for a man on the lam to hide." Chris probed the wound of her brother. "Where else would Ryan go?"

"Not here for long. I told him he isn't welcome."

Lauren selected an apple from the bowl, then returned it and rose to go into the kitchen. "Do you take your coffee black?"

She didn't remember. Oddly, that annoyed him.

"A splash of cream, if you have it. Black, if all you have is skim milk."

"Please. Who insults good coffee with skim milk?" She warmed half-and-half in the microwave, poured it into two coffee-filled mugs and carried them to the table before she spoke again. "Ryan handles commercial real estate in Colorado. How could he be a drug smuggler in Texas? Besides that, I've seen his tax returns. He doesn't need the money."

"He's too rich to break the law?" Chris didn't bother to keep the sarcasm from his voice. "That isn't a very convincing defense."

"The evidence is circumstantial. No one ever caught him with drugs in his possession."

"If he isn't guilty, Lauren, why didn't he accept the plea bargain? And why did he run?"

Lauren stared into her coffee for so long Chris thought she wouldn't answer. Then she wrapped her hands around the mug commemorating a ten-year-old Christmas and gave him a direct look. "Prison scared him to death. He's not a fighter, even if some of his activities may be on the wrong side of the law. The idea of being separated from fresh air and open spaces scares him. The nights he's spent in jail while awaiting arraignment and bail still give him nightmares."

"He's not a fighter?" Chris stared at her, his own hands wrapped around a mug proclaiming Peace on Earth and Goodwill toward Men.

"He wouldn't even fight with me when we were children."

"Then how did he manage to overpower a courtroom security guard, steal his gun and evade capture this morning?"

Lauren gnawed on her lower lip.

Chris drank his coffee. It was high quality, as was everything surrounding Lauren Wexler since she had turned a school computer science project into a prosperous business. He could wait her out. Patience came with his job.

Across from him, Lauren sipped at her coffee, set down the mug, then picked it up immediately to sip some more. When Chris tried to hold her gaze, she turned her head toward the end of the great room, where the door led to the deck overlooking the lake. For a heartbeat, Chris thought she was simply avoiding his scrutiny. Then he heard the crunch of footfalls on the deck, the rattle of the door handle followed by a resounding thud. The door shuddered under the impact of someone trying to break into the house.

THREE

Chris reached for his weapon. He had forgotten it wasn't there. It had vanished somewhere during the moments when he and Lauren had headed for the house the first time. Or it had vanished with Lauren, and she had stashed it away somewhere when she said she was collecting the first-aid kit. Either way, the gun was gone. He had no way to protect Lauren or himself while someone slammed hard enough against the back door to make it shudder in its frame.

Chris glanced around the room for some sort of weapon. Other than chunks of wood too short and thick to use as clubs, nothing presented itself to him.

"Where is my gun?" Chris demanded, not expecting an answer.

"I don't know." Lauren gripped the edge of the table. "I felt it beneath you near the woodpile—"

"Ryan Delaney," a man shouted outside the door, "open this door if you know what's good for you."

"Don't—"

"Ryan isn't in here," Lauren shouted back before Chris could get out his warning for her to remain quiet.

"Come out, Delaney, if you want to keep your sister alive," another man yelled.

"He's not—"

Chris grasped Lauren's hand and headed for the steps. "You can't argue them into believing your brother isn't here."

"Wait." Lauren held back. "I should get my cell phone. I'll need it when we reach the road and have service."

"No time." Chris pounded up the steps, Lauren sprinting behind him in her moccasins. He hesitated for a moment at the landing, remembering the configuration of the house outside, and steered them toward the far bedroom.

Below, a window smashed. In moments, the men would manage to batter through the shutters.

Chris and Lauren dived into the bedroom. Once inside, he closed and locked the door, then started to drag the heavy chest of drawers across the room. His injured shoulder gave out, and his hand slipped from the edge, throwing him off balance. He stumbled and would have fallen, tripping on the edge of the throw rug, but Lauren's arm encircled his waist and held him upright, held him close.

For a heartbeat, the contact felt right, natural. Then he got his feet under him again and shook off her touch. "Help me push this."

"Yes, sir." She saluted and marched around to the other end of the dresser.

"Please."

She shoved the chest toward him. He pulled. Together, they slid the solid oak piece across the rug to block the door.

A crash and thud below warned the men had entered the house. Their shouts of "Where are you, Delaney?" confirmed Chris's fears.

Lauren bowed her head. "God, please help Ryan if he is out there."

"Help him what?" Pain and frustration sharpened Chris's tone. "Help him avoid capture? Help him get to Canada to elude justice?"

"If my brother is guilty, I don't expect him to elude justice." Lauren's tone was as icy as the sleet outside as she raised her head, but the glow of a night-light on one wall didn't provide enough illumination for Chris to read her expression.

"'If'? Lauren, he's a fugitive. And now—" Chris broke off.

No sense in repeating the same arguments. She would never believe her big brother capable of armed transport of narcotics with the intent to sell. She had always thought the sun rose and set on Ryan, who did not in the least deserve her adulation, except that he had always treated her like a princess when the rest of her family neglected her.

"Do you think an innocent man would have thugs like these after him?"

Footfalls thudded on the steps.

"That chest won't hold them for long." Lauren's face was pale, her pupils dilated.

"It only needs to hold them long enough for us to get out the window."

"Out the window? But we're not dressed for this weather."

"We're not bulletproof either." Chris snatched up

an afghan from the foot of the bed. "Wrap this around you."

"You—"

"I'm fine."

He wouldn't be for long in this kind of cold, but a little frostbite sounded better than facing these men unarmed.

"We can get into the attic from here. If we open the window, they'll think we left that way while we're still inside."

"We'd be trapped if they decided to hang out here, but misdirecting is a good idea. We can try to make them think we went into the attic. Can you pull that ladder down?" Chris strode across the room to the window and flung back the shutters. Sleet pinged against the glass, a substance nearly as deadly as the men bellowing and banging throughout the house. Neither of them wore outdoor clothing. Nonetheless, he shoved up the sash and leaned out. Pellets of ice struck his skin like a thousand frozen hypodermic needles. He winced where the wood had battered his scalp what felt like hours ago. "How far down from the garage roof to the ground?"

"Ten feet."

"Can you get yourself down that far? With the snow, the landing shouldn't be too rough."

"I'll be all right if you will."

Chris hoped and prayed she was right. He didn't want to see her hurt, especially with someone following them.

Following.

"Let's go, then," Chris said.

With ease, they stepped over the low windowsill and onto the garage roof. Their footfalls crunched through the sleet-covered snow, no doubt leaving a trail the men could follow without light. No help for it. They were committed to their route now.

"I'll go first." Before he could stop her, Lauren flopped onto her belly and eased herself over the lip of the roof.

A thud and gasp followed her escape. Chris didn't waste time asking if she was all right. He mimicked her movements, landing in a snowdrift that wasn't as soft as it looked. Winded, pain shooting through his shoulder and head, he lay motionless for a heartbeat—then two— all too aware of Lauren gasping beside him, but unable to talk for several moments and ask her if she was hurt.

And above them, a gunshot split the night.

"They're going to get into that room soon." Chris hauled himself to his feet and reached to help Lauren up. "Let's get inside the garage."

"I'll drive. I know the terrain." Lauren grasped his hands and hauled herself to her feet.

For a heartbeat, their eyes met and held in the snow-brightened night. Then Lauren jerked her hands free and spun toward the garage's back door.

Lauren shoved open the rear door of the garage. "We have to take the snowmobile."

"Why not the Jeep?" Chris asked.

"The key is in my purse inside the house. I should have grabbed it. I didn't think—"

"No time for that now. We'll take the snowmobile."

On a hook beside the entrance to the house hung a key to the snowmobile. If ever she needed proof Ryan was in serious danger, it was the presence of the key and vehicle on runners. Ryan would have taken the snow-mobile if he'd had the time. He knew she never locked the garage and always kept the key handy in the event a hunter or winter hiker got lost, injured or snowbound and needed to reach shelter. So typical of her nature—risk someone stealing the contents of her garage if leaving the attached building open might save a life.

Cold slipping through her limbs to freeze her stomach into a ball of ice, Lauren tossed aside the tarp covering the snowmobile and started to straddle the seat.

"Wait." Chris rested a restraining hand on her shoulder. "The minute you fire this up, they are going to hear it. We need to be ready to fly out of here."

"It's already facing the door and can handle a few feet of concrete."

"But the door's electric, isn't it?"

"There's an override switch since I can't get the remote out of the Jeep without the keys."

"Where?"

Lauren indicated the door to the house. "Beside that."

As though poised to sprint, Chris balanced on the balls of his feet for a moment—a moment during which more shouts and crashes reverberated from inside. From the sound of it, the men were wrecking her house, her beautiful, private haven that had ceased being a sanctuary the instant someone shot at her and Ryan.

Her heart twisted. No time to worry about that.

Chris sprang off the balls of his feet and headed for the override switch. "Fire up the machine when I flip this switch, and head for the door. The instant it's high enough, get outside."

"But you—"

"I'll catch up with you."

She hoped he could make the dash and leap with his wounded shoulder and head. She hoped she could drive with her fingers numb from cold. The afghan wasn't much help, though better than nothing.

"Go." Chris flipped the switch.

The door motor whirred to life. Lauren leaped aboard the snowmobile, released the brake and shoved the key into the ignition. The engine roared. She released the choke, and the machine surged forward toward doors not quite high enough. Her numb fingers fumbled with the brake, stopping her momentum seconds before she slammed into the steel garage door. In front of her, the panel seemed to creep up at half its normal rate. If the men hadn't heard the engine fire yet, they would figure it out soon enough, or find her and Chris's footprints on the garage roof, or…

"Calm down." Chris's voice was deep and calm behind her.

He had swung his leg over the snowmobile seat without her realizing it.

"You're going to hyperventilate."

He wrapped his arms around her. The action was necessary to keep him aboard once they started forward, yet the contact felt like comfort.

She prayed for protection and mercy on them both, especially Chris. Once they headed out, his back would be vulnerable to gunshots, and he had left his Kevlar vest in Ryan's room.

No wonder he hadn't argued about her driving.

"I should have opened this door by hand." Despite him telling her to be calm, Chris's voice now held an edge.

Behind them, the door to the house opened and someone shouted, "They're getting away."

"Go, go, go!"

Lauren didn't need Chris's shout in her ear to release the brake and send the machine sailing beneath the half-risen door. They ducked just in time. The bottom edge caught the frame of the windshield. No worries. They were through.

"Go down the drive," Chris shouted. "And keep your head as low as you can."

But they couldn't take the most direct route to the road. A monstrous black truck stood sideways across the course.

And behind them, gunfire exploded over the roar of the snowmobile's engine. They swayed to the side to balance against the sharp turn needed to avoid crashing into the truck. And a bullet barely missed them, hitting the frame of the windshield. It bent but didn't break.

Lauren's heart stopped for so long she feared it had broken. "We're trapped."

"Head for the woods," Chris called into her ear.

His voice, firm, decisive, settled her heart to a fast but regular rhythm. She nodded and focused on the glare of light on the snow. That light pinpointed their direction, but then, so did the roar of the engine. Unless the men after Ryan, and now them, had a snowmobile as well, she and Chris might find shelter in the woods.

Had Ryan, after he had been to the cabin?

Her throat closed at the idea of her big brother freezing to death in the snow and trees, the sleet and wind. He had too likely chosen to follow their father's path, whose business practices Lauren never trusted to be legal except on the surface. Yet Ryan had been a rock to her when her parents split up, when she was afraid of her own shadow, when she chose computer science as a career path rather than social work as her grandmother had once hoped or business as her father wanted. Ryan had encouraged her to follow her dreams.

Lord, save his life tonight and forever.

It was a familiar prayer for her brother, stronger now than ever.

Ahead of her, her headlight beam caught the hulking pillars of trees. She steered between them, and another bullet crashed into the windshield from a weapon powerful enough the blast shattered the safety glass.

"Don't stop."

Lauren didn't need Chris's command to keep going, despite icy pellets and wind now dashing full in her face without the benefit of wearing goggles. She squinted against the impact and kept the machine moving, taking a turn between two trunks so close together Chris had to clamp his legs hard against the sides of the seat to not smash his knees. He didn't complain. He understood what she was doing.

"Good job." His approval was like a breath of warm air pushing back the cold.

Stupid. Stupid. Stupid her. That bullet had shattered her windshield, not the shield around her heart that had once loved this man with his arms encircling her.

"Where are we going?" She turned her head long enough to project her query to Chris—and cried out.

A solitary light blazed through the trees. A moment later, she caught the roar of another snowmobile.

FOUR

With his arms around her, Chris felt more than heard Lauren's gasp of alarm over the roar of the engine. The double roar. Two engines. He risked a glance back, saw the bobbing light behind them.

"Head for the road." He tilted his head so his lips grazed her ear. "As best you can."

She nodded, shaking all over. He wished he could drive, grab the handlebars and send them flying through the trees. Foolishness. They could move no faster without the risk of slamming into a tree.

"They can't shoot while dodging trees with us." He spoke as much to reassure himself as her.

His still-aching back felt like a giant bull's-eye. Which was why he would have insisted Lauren drive even if she hadn't been more familiar with the landscape. She was safer in front of him, his body shielding her from any assault from behind.

He couldn't shield her from the freezing rain turning to snow, from whipping branches, from the impact that seemed inevitable at any second as trees seemed to leap into the beam of their headlight. A swerve to the left, a jerk to the right avoided collision with a spruce, a birch, a maple sapling. Roots popped from the ground, and they sailed over them, hitting the earth with a teeth-jarring slam, tilting. As one, they leaned the other way, preventing the machine from spilling them onto the snow like litter for the men behind them to collect.

Too close behind them.

On one swing to the right to avoid a massive evergreen, Chris caught the glint of the other headlight from the corner of his eye. Closer than before. Either the men knew these woods or they were simply following Chris and Lauren's light. Likely the latter. Dangerous to have it on. More dangerous to travel without it.

"How far to the road?" Chris shouted into her ear.

Lauren shrugged. "Mile" was what he thought he heard, her voice drifting back on the wind.

Maybe she said *miles*. Either would be too far if their pursuers gained on them further.

Entirely possible. The path lay broad and straight ahead of them, glowing white despite the clouds and falling precipitation. If Lauren could drive faster, so could the men behind them. If their machine was more powerful—

Chris brought that thought up short. Focus on the moment, on the straightaway as long as it lasted.

On not shivering himself off the seat.

He glanced back. The light in pursuit glared yellow, a monster with a single eye. Not nearer, not farther. Behind them, coming on in relentless pursuit.

"Right or left?" Lauren's voice, loud enough to hear above the engine, held a note of panic.

Chris jerked his head forward. The path split in a Y. "You don't know?"

"This isn't my land anymore and I've lost my sense of direction in the dark."

So had Chris.

Some lawman he made, depending on a civilian to get him out of a jam.

"Right. Cut the light and turn right."

That might delay the men behind them for a moment or two. Long enough to get Lauren and him to the road and his SUV before the cold killed them faster than the men with guns.

They had been heading north. The road was to the east. Right should take them east if all their swerving and dodging hadn't turned them around.

The path remained wide. Surely a good sign. Hikers in summer and snowmobilers and cross-country skiers in winter would want wide, cleared paths.

He glanced back again. Nothing. The men weren't following for the moment.

"They didn't turn this way." Chris spoke in Lauren's ear so she could hear him. "At least not yet."

She nodded and flicked the headlight on again. A mixture of snowflakes and freezing rain reflected the thin yellow beam like a beaded curtain, more hindrance than help. Before Chris could suggest they might be safer without the light, Lauren switched it off. Now the world glowed eerily white with dark slashes of trees falling away on either side.

Falling farther away on either side.

The road. They must have reached the road.

The runners tilted up ahead of them, and the engine whined with the strain to climb an embankment. Chris held Lauren tightly, prepared for a sudden drop into a ditch. If that happened, the snow should cushion the fall. They would be all right. He could keep her safe.

Rocks rattled beneath the runners, shifting, tumbling away on either side, behind, before. Not the edge of the road. No rocks lined the highway.

"I can't stop now," Lauren cried.

Chris tensed, prepared to drag Lauren and himself clear if they flipped over.

They remained upright. With a crack like rifle fire and a thud that rattled every bone in his body and scrambled his brains, they landed on a solid surface.

Chris twisted around to see if the others had pursued them this way after all, had spotted them through the ice and snow, had risked a shot. Nothing behind them but the patter of the falling sleet. No sound of a following snowmobile. Little sound from theirs. Lauren had cut the engine. It settled into silence with a *tick, tick, tick*.

"Chris, come on." Lauren was scrambling off the machine and tugging on his arm. "We have to get out of here."

As the ticking and crackling continued, Chris realized what it was, understood the reason for Lauren's panic.

They had landed on the lake, and the ice was breaking beneath them.

Somewhere on their mad flight, Lauren had lost her sense of direction. Numb with cold inside her flannel shirt and the heavy but inadequate afghan, Lauren scrambled up the pile of rocks someone had left at the lakeshore, Chris behind her, and tried to think where her reasoning had gone wrong. She had turned west when she thought she'd headed east. That meant she had turned south when she'd thought she was headed north.

"I'm sorry." She slumped onto the rocks still poised at the edge of the water and speared her fingers through her hair.

At least she thought she did. She could barely feel them.

"Get up, Lauren." Chris grasped her arms and lifted her to feet that felt more frozen than the lake. "We can't stay here. We'll freeze to death in minutes."

"I know, but I'm so disoriented now, I'm not sure which way the road is."

"Back the way we came and along the other arm of that Y?"

"You mean the way those men after us—" she huddled deeper into the snow-encrusted afghan "—those men after Ryan went?"

"I think so. But we have to risk it. We have to keep moving." They started down the trail they had taken. "We must get to the road."

"And if they are on the road?" Lauren pictured that other snowmobile headlight pinpointed on the SUV Chris had said he left parked along the highway.

All those men had to do was wait for them.

"Should we go back to the house?" Lauren asked.

The warm stove. Hot chocolate, dry clothes.

A smashed window and broken-down doors. The quiet haven of her lakeside retreat had been ruined.

Ryan, why did you come to me?

To deliver the USB drive to someone he trusted.

Then her smashed-up house and Ryan's wound must not be in vain. She needed to help Chris get them to safety before they turned into human Popsicles.

What of Ryan wandering the woods on foot? He had been dressed warmly, right for this climate and weather. *Odd, that.* He must have had the clothes stashed somewhere he could get to without being caught, which meant not in his house, or he had bought them. Or he had help. Still, he had been wounded. He could have fallen, frozen to death, not to be found until spring.

Lauren shivered and lifted one end of the afghan. "Wrap this around you. It isn't much, but it's better than what you have on."

"It's less for you."

"I'll have a lot less if you freeze to death because I won't share."

"Ah, Lauren." A huskiness entered his voice.

He brushed his fingers across her cheek, an action she saw more than felt with her face numb like she had been shot full of Novocain, but a shiver having nothing to do with the cold still traveled through her. Remembrance of their past love for one another. Memories of his ability to show gentleness when she had known too little before him. Fear that he could break her heart all over again.

Not getting to warmth and safety should be a greater fear than her foolish heart. She was the one who rejected him with good reason—provable reasons now.

"May I?" Chris held out his arm.

It was a personal thing to do under most circumstances, a gesture between family members, friends, couples. They were none of those, but they were two people needing to preserve what little warmth remained in their bodies. Walking with their arms around one another made the most sense, as long as the path allowed them to remain side by side.

"Yes, of course." She voiced her approval.

His arm around her shoulders and hers around his waist, they set out on the trail back the way they had come. The sleet had left a top crust their moccasins would have trodden without difficulty if the freezing rain had not turned to powdery snow. In minutes, they were maneuvering through ankle-deep sand in slippers. Snow caked on their suede footgear. Each of Lauren's feet felt as though they weighed twenty pounds. Movement made the numbness leave her body. In its place, her legs began to ache with the effort of each step.

"I haven't been spending enough time on the treadmill." She tried to make a joke.

"That makes two of us."

Two of us. The two of them. But they weren't two. They were one and one, not even one plus one.

Chris stopped. "Hold this branch for balance and I'll see what I can do to get the snow off your slippers."

Lauren gripped a stout branch jutting over the path. Chris crouched at her feet and removed one moccasin, gave it a hard slap against the tree trunk, then replaced it on her foot before repeating the process with the other.

"That'll help for a little while," he said.

"Do you need my help?" Lauren started to ask.

But Chris was already using the tree trunk to knock the accumulated crystals from his footwear.

Shoes clear for the moment, they set out again, trying to match strides when Chris had nearly a foot of height on Lauren, trying to make as little noise as possible. Lauren listened for the purr of an engine in the woods, peered through the flakes sticking to her lashes for a glimpse of a headlight, for a break in the trees.

She saw the break in the trees first, the widening of the trail indicating where the path had split into a Y.

"Do we take the other arm or go back the way we came?" She didn't trust her own judgment after losing her sense of direction earlier.

"You trust me to decide after I directed you wrong before?" Chris's voice held an edge.

"We'll both make a decision and see if we agree?"

"Wait here." Chris tramped forward, vanishing behind a white veil.

She would recommend the wider path because she was cold and tired and it looked easier.

Trying to locate Chris by sound, Lauren snuggled her face into the afghan and caught a familiar scent. Clean. Crisp. Masculine. So comforting.

Except it was Ryan's scent, not Chris's. Chris was wearing Ryan's shirts. Ryan had always been there to give her comfort when Chris left for his new job with the United States Marshals Service, and before that when her stepmother, her father's third wife, walked away, when their father went to prison, when her mother abandoned her.

What did Chris smell like? They had been engaged. Surely she had been near enough to him to inhale his particular scent. That she couldn't recall left a hollowness inside her, a loss.

"Lauren?"

She jumped. "I'm still here."

He snorted, a sound more derisive than amused, and merely said, "I think we should go back down the main trail. Either one should lead us to the road or to your house and help us get our bearings. And the main trail offers shelter if we hear them coming."

Wordlessly, they continued as they had before, both wrapped in the afghan, stepping with care to avoid collecting too much snow in their slippers. Around them, the woods popped and cracked, branches breaking under the weight of ice and snow. The falling flakes thickened, silent now, too cold for ice. Walking warmed Lauren. If she kept her head down, her hair, loosened from its braid, sheltered her face. The numbness left her cheeks. Chris had to be suffering with his short hair and exposed ears. She glanced up. In the glow of moonlight she saw he had pulled the collar of the flannel shirt over his ears and tucked his chin into the neckline buttoned all the way up.

"It can't be much farther." She spoke out of hope. "The lake isn't more than a mile off the highway. As long as we are going in the right direction."

They were not going in the right direction. They edged around a curve in the trail and the world opened before them, the lake to their right, her house to the left.

Until that moment, she had been able to keep going. Right then, she wanted to lie down and cry.

"We were just going round in a circle."

"Half circle." His tone and the gentle squeeze of his arm on her shoulders said he was trying to make a joke to lighten the mood.

"I suppose we can't go back inside." She knew the answer.

"They may have left someone there."

Light shone through the slats of the shutters. A lack of smoky smell suggested the fire had gone out, but the men had either allowed at least one of their gang to remain in the shelter of solid walls or closed up with care.

"So much for my full propane tanks." She attempted

a joke too. "Merry Christmas to the thugs inside enjoying my heater."

"My SUV has a great heater. We can get there now."

"How without them seeing us?"

"We stay inside the tree line."

They skirted the clearing just inside the line of trees so no one could see them from the house. When they reached the driveway, they paused. The monstrous truck that had blocked their passage earlier was gone. Beside Lauren, Chris tensed.

"What's wrong?" Even her murmur sounded like a shout in the quiet.

"I just thought..." He trailed off.

Lauren waited.

Chris nudged her forward. She went, but prompted, "Yes?"

"If they found my Jeep, we may have nothing to go to once we reach the road."

Lauren stopped. "Then should we go back to the house and take our chances there?"

"I think we should stick to the original plan."

Lauren nodded and trudged on. Half a mile. No more. Twenty-six hundred feet or so, less in steps. She had surely walked farther along that trail.

The trail had been easy. Edging along trees and breaking through shrubbery was harder. If she survived, she would clear out this area, make the trees easier to pass through. Wasn't that better in the event of a forest fire anyway?

Ah, a fire. How she would love to sit beside a fire. Cold was tolerable if a body knew warmth was imminent.

Chris's SUV would have a heater. She would not consider that the men after them, after Ryan, had damaged it.

She would imagine the two of them steaming like dumplings and fogging up the windows as the car's heater warmed the air.

"Where did you park?" Lauren thought to ask.

"In someone's driveway. I hiked in. I didn't want the engine to announce my approach."

So Ryan wouldn't be warned if he was there.

Her heart felt as heavy as her moccasins. Chris was helping her get to safety now, but he was first and foremost after her brother. It was his duty. The moment she was safe and sound somewhere, he would rejoin the manhunt for Ryan.

He would leave her.

Lauren's throat closed. She couldn't even sigh with relief when she saw the highway through the trees, a dark ribbon against the white wrapping of the snow.

The cleared area indicated the plows and salt trucks had passed that way recently, so recently the plow's flashing red light shone to the south. And to the left the truck that had blocked her driveway earlier crouched at the edge of the highway, its headlights reaching out like laser beams that would catch them in the glare if they stepped onto the road.

FIVE

If he had had his weapon, he could've shot out those headlights and given Lauren and himself the cover of the night and the storm to run across the road and up the deserted driveway where he had parked his Jeep. But his weapon was…somewhere. If Lauren had it, he didn't know where she'd stowed it. And yet he didn't know how it could have disappeared so swiftly from the end of the deck if she hadn't taken it.

No sense speculating on that now. They had to get out of sight, cross the road, find transportation before they died of exposure. Chris knew he was dangerously close to being too cold except along his side, where Lauren still stood close. Leaned against him, in truth. She must be exhausted. He was. Sleep sounded far too nice at the moment.

A true sign of hypothermia—sleepiness.

"We need to move." Chris drew Lauren into the trees. "If we can get behind them, we have a chance of crossing the road without anyone seeing us."

"We can't go that way inside the tree line. There's a culvert under the road. The water is probably frozen solid, but we can't risk it."

"I'm glad I'm with you."

To learn that, he meant. He hoped she understood that was all he meant. He would much rather have been alone.

That's not true. His mother's and sister's voices rang in his head. *You're twenty-nine years old. You shouldn't be alone anymore.*

He wished they were wrong. He wished their admonitions to settle down and marry hadn't popped into his head at that moment.

"We'll have to run for it," Chris said.

"Maybe no one is in the truck?" Lauren's tone sounded hopeful. "They didn't try to shoot at us or run us down when we stepped out of the trees."

"It's entirely possible they just left the truck there after bringing it out of your driveway."

"But unlikely.

"Or a moment of not paying attention." Lauren's sigh was audible above the wind.

"We just don't know how many men are here. At least two," Chris added.

"We'll run across the road, then." Lauren stepped away from Chris, leaving the afghan behind on his shoulders. "I'm ready."

The road was only a two-lane highway. It looked like a major interstate of at least ten lanes with those headlights glaring and expanding against the curtain of white spilling from the sky.

Chris draped the afghan around his neck like an oversize scarf and grasped Lauren's hand. "When I get to three, run as fast as you can. Okay?"

"Yes, sir."

"Ready. One." Chris stepped from the trees. "Two. Three."

They began to sprint. Gracelessly. Clumsily. A flat-footed slap of wet suede moccasins on blacktop rather than the light pad of high-tech rubber in a proper dash. Chris shortened his stride for Lauren's lesser inches. Despite the recent passage of plows and salt trucks, the road's surface bore another coating of snow turning to slush as slick as oil. Speed was merely a want, a hope. If another vehicle approached, Chris and Lauren would be two more statistics on someone's accident report.

Chris glanced to the right, seeking headlights. Snow and darkness met his gaze. To their left, the truck's headlights glared, flared to high beams.

Someone was in the truck. Someone started the engine. Its rumble split the night. Gears shifted.

The trees looked a hundred miles away. Chris yearned to leap faster. His feet slipped in the snow and ice trying to cling to the blacktop. Beside him, Lauren dropped to one knee with a gasp, but was up and hurtling ahead before Chris had time to react.

The roar of the engine sounded louder. Chris didn't risk glancing back. A moment's inattention to the pavement increased the likelihood of slipping on black ice. Falling. Not getting up before those oversize tires bore down upon them...

The edge of the road passed beneath their soles, driving them against a snowbank from the plow's passage.

"Climb."

A stupid thing to say. They could do nothing else.

They climbed up, up and over the hard-packed snow and ice tossed to the side of the road. Beyond it more trees rose, their branches laden with white and crystals in the sun-bright glare of the headlights. Chris lifted Lauren and propelled her over the last of the snowbank and behind a tree. Seconds after he joined her, the truck slammed to an abrupt halt, tires buried in the side of the road.

"They'll get out," Lauren was gasping.

"Let them."

"What?" In the radiant light from headlights and snow pouring through the tree branches, her eyes shone huge and dark, her cheeks pink from cold or exertion or both.

She was so pretty.

Chris drew them beneath a pine tree with branches hanging nearly to the ground. "We'll wait and see what they do. If it's just one man, I might be able to stop him."

"We'll freeze."

"We won't wait that long."

Chris wrapped them both in the afghan, and they waited, clenching their teeth to stop them from chattering, though no one could have heard it above the grumble of the truck engine. For too long, nothing happened. Just when Chris thought they needed to start creeping toward his SUV, a shadow passed before the headlights. Chris peered out from their hiding place in time to see the truck door was open and a man was headed into the trees. He held a cell phone in one hand and a gun in the other.

"You can't stop him," Lauren murmured in Chris's ear, her breath warm against his cold skin. "He's armed."

"I should be." Chris set his lips in a hard, thin line and watched the man.

He wore cold-weather gear, not an afghan.

Chris gave the afghan to Lauren and started to rise.

She wrapped both hands around his arm and held him back. "Wait. Do you think we could take his truck?"

Chris didn't like the thought that sprang into his head. *Leave it to a lady with Delaney blood to think of breaking the law.* It wasn't fair. To his knowledge, assisting her brother was the first law Lauren had broken, and he wasn't yet sure how much she had helped Ryan escape. Besides, these were extenuating circumstances.

"I don't mean for long." Lauren's words seemed as though she'd read his thoughts. "I mean just to take us to your SUV. And it would slow this guy from coming after us."

"And his friend or friends." Chris conceded she had a good idea. "I suspect whoever else is with him is on their way."

"And we know they're armed, so this may be our only chance." Her hands shook on his arm. "I have to get out of the cold, and so do you, or I will be of no use—" She broke off.

She would be of no use to Ryan, he finished for her.

Ryan. Always Ryan. Her beloved brother got her love and loyalty.

But she was right in saying they couldn't remain in the cold any longer. If neither of them caught pneumonia or ended up with frostbite, it would be newsworthy.

"All right. Let's go."

Suggesting they borrow the truck—*take it*, she had actually said—was not the brightest move she had made that night. It wasn't the worst. Getting turned around in the woods and landing them on the lake was the worst.

Still, she felt Chris tense when she suggested stealing the truck.

Yes, stealing. That was how he saw it in his black-and-white, always by-the-book view of the world. One was either doing right or doing wrong. Taking the truck was doing wrong.

Yet there they were on another mad dash across the snow in moccasins. Chris lifted her through the open driver's-side door as though she weighed nothing and hadn't been indulging in too many Christmas cookies brought to her by her employees. Sugar cookies. Peanut butter blossoms. Mexican wedding cookies...

She was hallucinating from cold and fatigue and fear. Scrambling past the gearshift in their desperate attempt to get away from whoever wanted her brother, whoever was willing to shoot them to get to Ryan, all she could think about was the box of cookies left on her kitchen counter.

Right behind her, Chris swung into the driver's seat, slamming the door behind him with one hand and reaching for the brake with the other.

Something thumped into the back door. Bullets. "Duck," Chris shouted.

But Lauren was already down.

"Hang on. This is going to be bumpy."

"I didn't think. Do you know how to drive a standard shift?"

He threw the truck into Reverse.

Lauren bounced off the seat and grabbed the armrest to stop herself from smashing into the door and then the dashboard or windshield. *Bumpy* was right. They jounced off the snowbank and lurched onto the black-top. The truck fishtailed on the slushy surface. Before them, the headlights arced off snow, trees and an on-coming snowplow.

Lauren closed her eyes. She didn't want to witness the impact.

The truck jerked. Gears ground, then they surged forward.

"We're all right." Chris's voice was calm. Soothing. "For the moment."

"It feels like the inside of a toaster compared to outside." Lauren held her hands in front of the heater vent. She started to slip her feet from the soaked moccasins.

"Not yet. My Jeep isn't far."

"Won't it be snowed in by the plow?"

"It can handle little drifts like these."

Now she was relatively safe, Lauren noticed the piles on the side of the road weren't as high as she'd thought earlier. When the truck was chasing them, the snow-bank had felt like a mountain.

"I'm more concerned about ice on the windshield," Chris was saying. "That could take us some time to clear."

"But we have their truck."

"They still have a snowmobile."

How could she forget? They also, apparently, had cell phones—useless off the highway but highway reception was excellent.

Lauren huddled inside the afghan, willing it to absorb heat for the next plunge into the cold.

Which came all too soon. What seemed like seconds later, Chris pulled the truck as far to the side of the road as the plowed banks allowed and cut the engine and lights. He tucked the keys beneath the seat and pushed open the door. A blast of wind and snow smacked Lauren like a fist. She gasped, but clambered over the gearshift to slide out the open door.

"Where is your Jeep?"

"Up this driveway. Do you know the owners?"

"We met once last summer. They're from Illinois and don't get up here much."

"No lake on this side." Chris tucked his hand beneath her elbow to help her over the mound of snow at the foot of the driveway.

"They have a river."

"I prefer lakes."

"I remember."

They had been standing on the shore of Lake Michigan, the expanse of crystal-blue water stretching to the horizon beneath an equally blue sky, white sand eddying beneath their feet with each wave, when he proposed to her. Two weeks later, his father had been killed in the line of duty, and Chris made a decision that changed their lives, their love, a friendship of nearly two years.

Lauren could scarcely breathe. Suddenly, each inhalation felt like someone had replaced oxygen with icicles.

"It's only another hundred feet or so." Chris's voice was too energetic. "We can make it."

"Trying to convince me or yourself?" Lauren asked in a tone as brittle as the ice replacing her air.

"Both of us."

"Still truthful to the core." She half smiled despite cracked lips.

His honesty was one of the things she loved about him. Had loved about him. Now she had only one person in her life left to love—Ryan, the fugitive somewhere in the woods still, maybe. Wounded, maybe. Dead, maybe.

"I have a scraper and a brush and emergency supplies." Chris pressed the remote ignition.

With only a hint of a stutter, the engine fired up, promising warmth and escape—eventually.

"Do those supplies include a propane heater?" Lauren tried to joke.

"My snow boots and clothes."

"What a blessing for you." She couldn't find a fleck of humor this time.

"I can give you dry socks and a thermal blanket. And water."

"Even that much sounds good." Lauren leaned against the hood, savoring the first hint of warmth from the engine. "I'll start brushing the snow off."

Chris brought her a small broom for brushing snow off the windows, along with a shiny space blanket. He wrapped the latter around her instead of the soaked afghan. "I'll scrape."

They worked as a team, Lauren brushing snow off the windows and hood, Chris scraping the underlying ice. All the while, Lauren kept looking over her shoulder for headlights, for the shadow of a man passing across their lights. She strained to hear the sound of another vehicle, truck or snowmobile above the purr of the Jeep's engine. Or the crack of a gunshot.

She finished brushing off the SUV, including standing on the running board so she could reach the roof.

"Go ahead and get inside," Chris said when Lauren sent the last mini avalanche of snow cascading to the ground.

"Then you take this." She gave him the space blanket.

He hesitated, then accepted her gift. "I won't be much longer. They'll find us far too fast."

Lauren climbed into the passenger side of the Jeep. Already the powerful engine had begun to warm the air streaming from the heater vents. She wanted to curl up in the footwell beneath the dash and savor every iota of warmth blowing upon her. If she took off her sodden moccasins, her feet could warm. But if they had to run again, she might be without anything on her feet.

A pair of wool socks lay draped across the console in the stream of hot air from an upper vent. They would be too big. She didn't care. She snatched them up and pulled them onto toes that appeared dangerously pale in light from the dash. With the socks on and her feet pressed to the lower vent, her toes felt cherished at last.

Outside, Chris scraped away at the cloud of ice on the windshield, creating an opening just large enough for safety, then moved to the back for the same treatment. The rasp of the plastic blade against glass set Lauren's teeth on edge. Guilt. She was growing warm. He was outside in the cold. If the men found them, she was far safer than he was.

Because of her. Because he had known Ryan would come to her.

Which was why she had felt the need to break off their engagement five years earlier. She couldn't drag Chris down, risk his career, when she knew her father was out of prison but still walking along the edge of criminal behavior, with her knowing he would cross it again. She didn't think Ryan had. But maybe that was wishful thinking and not reality. At least it definitely was now, with what Ryan had done in that courtroom.

The driver's-side door popped open. Chris tossed the scraper onto the floor behind his seat and climbed in.

"Thank you for the socks. My feet are warm now."

"I'm glad."

Chris put the SUV into gear and headed out of the driveway. "Put on your seat belt."

Lauren grabbed for the shoulder harness. A moment after she clicked the lock on the seat belt, they hit the snowbank, slamming over it onto the road, and slid on black ice across the highway to the other lane. Clear. Thankfully. A scream crammed into Lauren's throat. She tried to hold it back. Failed.

"I got it." Chris's extra soothing tone was more irritating than calming.

"You should know better than to drive that fast when you know the pavement is icy." The words burst from Lauren in unchecked anger.

And Chris laughed. "You sound like my mother."

Or a wife.

Lauren pressed herself back against the seat and covered her face with her hands. She breathed into her palms. She would be calm. She wouldn't say anything else.

Chris, competent as ever, got the Jeep under control and headed in the right direction—at what felt like a snail's pace—to the nearest town. To a sheriff's office. To a working telephone. They would say goodbye there.

Lauren's hands fell to her lap. If they had only a few more minutes together, she needed to say something to Chris one more time. But before she got out the "I'm sorry" she intended, she caught a flash of light in the rearview mirror.

A snowmobile was streaking down the highway behind them and gaining.

SIX

"Why are they following us on the snowmobile?" Lauren cried.

"They can go faster." Chris's face looked grim.

"But we can't."

"Not and stay on the road."

"Will they catch us? Will they shoot at us?"

"I don't know. Will you watch while I drive?"

"Of course."

Watch for what, she didn't know. Watch how close their pursuer or pursuers got. Watch for a muzzle flash.

She shivered despite the warming cabin.

The windows were fogging from the difference between temperature outside and in. Chris flicked on the defroster. The blast of cold air streaming off the windows felt like an insult to her senses. The sight of the snowmobile behind hurt her eyes. She couldn't tell if it was gaining. She hoped that whoever was driving was alone and too occupied with keeping up speed to fire at them. Better yet, that he was out of ammunition.

"Town is close." She made the announcement as much to encourage herself as Chris. "It's just a village.

But there's a sheriff's office and a diner and a couple of stores."

Only the sheriff's office would be open that late.

She glanced at the clock. She expected it to say midnight or later. The time said half past nine.

"Is your clock wrong?" she asked.

"It's right on time last time I checked. We really were only out there for less than an hour and a half."

"I thought—yikes." Half-turned to look out the rear window, she clutched at the seat back as Chris swerved right to pass a salt truck creeping along at half their speed.

The driver blared his horn.

"That won't keep them away from us for more than a few minutes, but it'll help," Chris said with a note of satisfaction.

Glancing back, Lauren saw only the salt truck, not the snowmobile. Ahead, she caught the lights at the widening of the road that was the nearest town. A gas station first, its lights brightly announcing it was still open after all. She wanted to beg Chris to stop. The station had a little store with hot coffee and chocolate.

"The sheriff's office is on the other side of the library," she said instead.

"This place has a library?"

"Tourists and summer residents want books and sometimes need computer and internet access. This time of year, it's open two days a week. Right there." She pointed to the old house now serving as the library and municipal offices. "There's parking behind."

Chris turned into a driveway not yet touched by plow or shovels. The Jeep's tires spun, sought tracti, gripped. The engine strained with all-wheel dri they were up a slight incline and pulling behind the building with the comfort of bright lights turning the snow and ice to wedding-cake frosting.

Reluctantly, Lauren pushed her feet into her cold, stiff moccasins and prepared for another dousing of the deep freeze outdoors.

"They won't let us in the back door," Lauren said.

"They will. Or are you forgetting my deputy US marshal credentials?"

"How could I forget that?" Her voice held a little more harshness than was polite. At that moment, she didn't care.

They were about to step into the world of law enforcement, where Chris was the good guy and she the sister of the felon. One of the enemies. Who the others were, she had no idea. Ryan probably did.

They slogged to the back door of the sheriff's station. Chris pressed the bell.

"Who is it?" An impossibly young-sounding voice came through the speaker.

"Christopher Blackwell, Deputy US Marshal." He held his credentials in front of the camera.

"Who's with you?" the disembodied voice asked.

"Lauren Wexler," Chris said.

"Is she under arrest?"

Chris glanced at Lauren, then back to the camera. "She has vital information to an investigation."

"___ he vital information," Lauren reminded ___ of the USB drive.

"___ n's information. I'm still waiting for

___ hed and opened her mouth to tell him

she knew nothing to help him. But maybe she did. She
hadn't taken time to think. She was too cold to think.

The *vroom* of a small engine cut through the quiet
night, and she whipped around in time to see a snowmobile speed into the parking lot, execute a one-eighty
so fast it nearly tipped onto one runner, then sail out
of the lot again.

"Are you going to let us in or not?" Chris's query
was sharp, demanding.

"Yes, sir." The door buzzed and a release clicked.

Chris palmed the door open and held it for Lauren to
go ahead of him. She stepped into a narrow hallway lit
with unstable fluorescent lights and smelling of burnt
coffee. At the far end, a young man in uniform stood
backlit against brighter lights.

"Deputy Davis, at your service." Lauren expected
him to bow. Instead, he held his hand out to Chris.
"What brings you out on a night like this?"

"It's a long story." Chris glanced to Lauren, then
back to the sheriff's deputy. "Are you the only one
here?"

"Right now, I am. Everyone else is out on accident
calls and a fire emergency." Davis glanced from one
to the other. "You two look half-frozen. Can I get you
some coffee or tea or cocoa? It's just the cocoa packets,
but they have marshmallows."

Lauren's lips twitched. She dared not look at Chris,
but caught his expression from the corner of her eye.
His lips were compressed as though he was trying not
to laugh.

This boy in uniform looked about sixteen.

"Some cocoa with marshmallows sounds perfect,"

Lauren said. "And maybe you have some blankets we can wrap up in until we dry?"

"Come sit at the front desk, ma'am. I got a space heater under it." The boy led the way to a desk bearing two telephones and a brand-new-looking computer. Billows of heat poured from the kneehole.

Lauren didn't need a second invitation to sit. She perched on the vinyl desk chair and immediately began to warm.

"Any chance I can use your telephone?" Chris asked. "We don't have our cell phones."

"Reception's bad here anyway." The officer glanced at the phones, each of which seemed to have four lines. "It's quieted down now. I guess it's all right, but maybe I should call the sheriff."

"You do that." Chris handed Davis his credentials. "He can check to make sure I'm legitimate."

Davis flushed. "Guess I should've done that."

"It's all right." Chris patted the boy's shoulder. "Being here alone on a night like this is a lot of responsibility."

Embarrassment turned to pride. "Yes, sir." He reached for the phone and tapped out a number he obviously knew by heart. The conversation was brief and mostly one-sided—the sheriff doing most of the talking. Davis nodded a great deal, as though he were on a video call. Then he hung up and nodded again toward Chris. "He says you can use his office."

"Thank you." And Chris was gone into another room. Through the glass-paneled door, Lauren saw him seated behind another desk like the one before her. She hoped it too held a space heater beneath. His voice was muffled, not a word distinct, but her ears burned. He was talking about her. If he wasn't, she would give up the cup of cocoa with marshmallows Davis set before her with a proud "I made it with milk, not water. Tastes better that way."

He then brought her a selection of aging magazines to read. *Game and Fish*, *Woods and Water* and *Michigan Golfer*. None were to her taste, but she pretended to read, while listening to the subdued rumble of Chris's voice go on and on behind the closed door and watching Davis pace the waiting room. The phone didn't ring once. Not a vehicle rolled past the front window. The three of them might have been alone in the world.

Then headlights flashed out front and an SUV roared up the driveway. Moments later, the back door banged open with a blast of frigid air. "Where are our visitors, Davis?" shouted a booming voice.

Lauren rose, expecting to find a man of equal size— great height and girth to match the basso profundo. The man who strolled into the front office was of no more than average height and weight, with beautiful golden-blond hair waving from beneath his hat. He, like Davis, looked far too young for his role, not more than a year or two older than Chris.

He yanked off his cap and held out his other hand to Lauren. "Sheriff Matt Davis."

"Davis?" Lauren glanced at the deputy.

"My nephew."

"Aha. I'm Lauren Wexler." Lauren shook the proffered hand.

"Own the lake house about five miles south."

"I do."

"So how'd you get picked up by a deputy US marshal?" Sheriff Davis glanced to his office.

"It's a really long story. Maybe he should tell you." She saw Chris rise and approach the office door.

He exited the office and introduced himself. "I'm happy to tell you what happened at Miss Wexler's house tonight, but first—"

What Chris said next flew right past Lauren while she recovered from him calling her Miss Wexler like she was a stranger. Or, worse, like he wanted to keep a barrier between himself and her.

"I only hesitate to say yes on the computer use," Davis was responding to Chris, "because our machines are new and I don't want a virus or something destroying them. Can you guarantee this USB drive doesn't have something destructive on it?"

Chris looked at Lauren. "What do you think?"

Chris asking her opinion about Ryan's USB drive made her feel like the nerdy high school girl getting asked to prom by the best pitcher on the baseball team— far better than the quarterback, since she didn't like football much. She nearly forgot to respond.

Because she was a fool to care.

"Lauren?" Chris prompted.

Realizing all three men were staring at her, she swallowed, licked her cracked lips. "I can't guarantee it. I have no idea what's on it. But I know how to take steps to protect your system."

"She's a computer genius," Chris explained.

Lauren ducked her head. "I wouldn't go that far, but I know a few tricks."

"As long as they work," Sheriff Davis said, "go right ahead. You can do that while Blackwell here tells me what this is all about and why knowing what's on that USB drive is so urgent."

Lauren held out her hand for the oblong plastic Ryan had given her a lifetime ago.

Chris fished it from the pocket of his sweatpants and laid it on her palm, then rested one hand on her shoulder. "No tricks if you don't want to join your brother in prison."

Fragile beneath the wool blanket, Lauren's shoulder went rigid under Chris's hand. He regretted his choice of words before she glanced at him, her eyes wide and bleak. "Did they catch him?"

"Not yet, but we will."

Chris had his doubts about whether or not anyone would catch Ryan except the men who were not law enforcement. Marshals were traveling to this area, where Lauren said she had last caught a glimpse of Ryan Delaney racing for the trees and trailing drops of blood on the snow. But the storm slowed everyone down. Calling people back from their Christmas vacations slowed everyone down. Not knowing the terrain slowed everyone down.

Nothing seemed to have slowed the men chasing Ryan and now Chris and Lauren. They knew Chris and Lauren were in the sheriff's station. All they needed to do was wait for them to leave and ambush them. And leave they must. Chris had to get Lauren someplace where she could wait for Ryan to be placed in custody, possibly in custody herself so she didn't help her brother. Chris needed to get into the extra winter gear in his Jeep and join the manhunt.

"How can I join Ryan in prison if he isn't there?" Lauren asked in her soft, low tones.

"By destroying the data on that USB drive."

Chris ignored the literal words of her question. She knew what he meant.

"Or warning him of our location while you're on the computer."

"I doubt he has internet access wherever he is. And you're probably not the only marshal looking for him."

Chris touched his fingertips to her cheek so she would keep looking at him. A mistake. Her skin had warmed. His fingers had warmed. Instead of feeling skin smooth like marble as he had in the woods, he now felt the satin texture of her complexion. He wanted to trace his fingertips across her cheekbones, her jawline, her stubborn round chin. He wanted to brush his thumb across her lips and—

He jerked his hand and gaze away. "Do you know where Ryan might be?"

"I've been thinking about it." She began to type into the computer, her fingers a blur on the keyboard. "He needs to be captured for his safety, and to explain why he escaped custody. I know you don't believe me, Chris, but I know it's true." She pushed the USB drive into a port.

Messages began to flash on the monitor. Password demands. Warnings.

"Of course it's password protected." Chris nearly groaned in frustration. "I can ship it to the nearest office with a computer forensics expert, but that'll take at least another day. We were hoping to email this information back to the Northern District of Illinois."

"I can break the password faster than anyone can deliver the USB drive, especially in this weather." Lauren spoke with calm confidence.

Chris didn't doubt her for a moment.

"What do you need?"

"Just this computer and some decent coffee. Some food wouldn't be a bad idea either."

"I'll see what I can do."

Chris left Lauren to her skills. From the smell in the station, decent coffee wasn't likely, so he was pleasantly surprised to learn they possessed a Keurig and the burnt-coffee odor stemmed from reheating cups in the microwave.

"I'll pay you back," he assured the sheriff and his deputy, then made Lauren a cup of coffee and plundered a cabinet of snacks for chips and a granola bar.

"I'll go down to the gas station for deli sandwiches," Deputy Davis offered. "They close up at eleven and practically give away what's left over at the end of the day."

"That's good of you, considering the weather." Chris produced his wallet and handed Davis some bills. "Buy whatever will get us all through the night."

The boy departed and Chris told the sheriff what was going on. Finished with his explanations, Chris began to pace the confines of the station. Sheriff Davis was in his office, talking to men patrolling the roads of the county, which seemed to include the drivers of a snowplow and a salt truck. "Have you seen a snowmobile or a pickup truck with extra large tires?" Davis asked each of them.

Chris had nothing to do. This wasn't his jurisdiction. He couldn't give orders. He got his information secondhand. He couldn't help Lauren. He had good computer skills, but they were utilitarian for everyday usage, not specialized like hers.

Deputy Davis returned with enough food to get ten

people through the night. Cold cuts, rolls, cheese, potato salad, chicken noodle soup, brownies. Chris poured some soup into a cup, made Lauren a sandwich and set everything beside the computer. She nodded her thanks, but never took her eyes off the monitor. He wasn't sure she really knew the food was there, but when he looked in on her later, she had even managed to consume the potato salad despite it requiring a fork.

"My little brother gets like that," Deputy Davis said, gazing at Lauren, "but I never saw a girl be into computers."

"She has been since long before I knew her."

Machines are always around, she had told him once. *You don't expect them to care about you, so they can't hurt you by stopping.*

As he had.

Except he hadn't stopped loving her until she left him with accusations that he had abandoned her.

He hadn't. He had abandoned his work in law in exchange for law enforcement. She wanted nothing to do with a law enforcement officer of any branch.

For the reason stretching before them. Her brother was a criminal. Chris was the one who would have to arrest him if he found Ryan first.

Telling himself he was curious about Lauren's progress with getting to the USB drive's data, and knowing in his heart he didn't quite trust her not to contact her brother, Chris stood behind her chair and stared at the monitor. The strings of characters meant nothing to him, but he remained silent so as not to break Lauren's concentration.

"The security on this device is tight." She volunteered the information. "I've broken two passwords so far."

"How many layers of passwords are there?"

"I have no way of knowing. This could be the last or we could be looking at another five or more."

"Why so many?"

"For this very reason. Us getting ahold of the USB drive. Ryan getting it. Anyone who isn't supposed to have it getting ahold of it." She rested her elbows on the desk and speared her fingers through her hair. "I wouldn't be surprised if half a dozen people were supposed to be present to open these files and each person had their own password."

"How long will it take you to crack the passwords?"

"As long as it takes." Her tone was sharp, impatient.

She rubbed her eyes. Dark circles like bruises marred her creamy complexion.

Chris shoved his hands into his pockets to stop himself from smoothing away a crease between her arching eyebrows. "More coffee?"

"Yes, please."

Chris started to turn toward the break room and coffee maker.

"Chris?" Lauren touched his arm.

He glanced back, half smiled.

"I'm sorry I snapped at you. This is my brother's future on the line."

"And my career."

He hadn't let himself think about that until this moment, but the truth glared at him like that pickup truck's high beams. If he failed to bring in Ryan Delaney, he wouldn't be outright accused of not doing due diligence in his job, but people, important people, would wonder if he had let his former fiancée's brother go free. He envisioned a future of being pushed out of promotion after promotion, until he was little more than a courthouse guard running ladies' purses through the metal detector eight hours a day.

"Which is more important, Chris?" Lauren's question was barely audible in the quiet room.

He just looked at her. She knew the answer without him saying it. Ryan was a criminal. How could his freedom from justice be more important than Chris's future in the US Marshals Service? Lauren loved her half brother, and yet she must realize he had proved he wasn't worth the sacrifice of her relationship with Chris.

Without a word, she returned her attention to the computer and began to click the keys.

Chris headed for the break room again, made coffee for Lauren and himself, then began to pace.

Around four o'clock in the morning, the back door of the station flew open on a gust of cold but dry air and three more deputies entered. They fell on the food in the refrigerator and began to tell tales of their night's adventures.

Besides tending to small vehicular accidents and a minor house fire, they had relit the pilot on an elderly lady's stove and rescued a cat from someone's roof. But they hadn't found the snowmobile the salt truck driver complained about. Nor had they seen the pickup with oversize tires. Lauren's house was shut up tight and dark, save for the broken door and damaged shutter.

"We found some bullet holes too and managed to collect some lead for analysis," another deputy reported.

If Lauren heard from her desk, she made no indication.

"And someone knocked down her antenna," the first speaker reminded them. "Couldn't tell in the dark with all the snow, but I think they must have had to climb onto the roof and take it down."

That got Lauren's attention. Her head snapped around, her eyebrows arched nearly to her hairline. "Why?" She blinked and grimaced. "Dumb question. Obviously, I wasn't supposed to have satellite phone service either."

"Who took out the antenna? Ryan or the men after him?" Chris held her gaze.

She shook her head and returned to the computer.

At 6:05 a.m. exactly, Lauren flung up her hands in a victory sign and let out a "Woot."

Chris was at her side in an instant. "You made it through all the passwords?"

"Six of them, and that's the good news."

"What's the bad news?" Chris picked up his cue.

"All the data is in code."

"Computer code?"

"No, cypher code." She tilted the monitor so he could read the gibberish on the screen. "But I expect you all have people who can break code. We can transmit it to them."

"If we don't, some agency does. Let me call my boss and find out where to send this."

Chris made the call. He passed the instructions to Lauren, who transmitted the data through as secure a channel as she could muster, which Chris figured was rather good, computer security being her passion in life.

Sheriff Davis took the USB drive and locked it in the safe they used as an evidence locker.

"Now what?" Lauren asked.

"I get you someplace secure and join the hunt for your brother."

"By *secure*, do you mean a jail cell?" Lauren asked.

"If that's where you'll be safest, yes."

SEVEN

Lauren couldn't breathe. The idea of being locked in a cell sent her head spinning. That Chris would put her in jail under the guise of her safety was unthinkable, despicable. Crushing.

"I'm not a criminal," she managed to gasp out.

"But you have their information now."

"I don't. Please believe me. I don't know any more than you do."

"So you didn't try to break the code?"

"Break the code?" That loosened her tongue. "I'm a software engineer, not a cryptologist. I know a wholly different kind of code. I'm not even good at puzzles."

"Except for jigsaw puzzles and Scrabble."

And several other snowy- or rainy-day activities played on a small table for two or maybe four. They had often been evenly matched at numerous board games and played them by the hour, sometimes joined by his mother and sister.

"You were the one who excelled at crossword puzzles," Lauren pointed out.

She shouldn't have. He shouldn't have brought up all those joyful hours of putting puzzles together or playing board games. It had been a happier, more carefree time, when her lawless father didn't matter to their lives. Once Chris's father, a prison warden, was murdered and Chris changed careers, their lives, their love, became a jigsaw puzzle knocked to the floor with several crucial pieces crushed beyond recognition.

Trust was one significant piece, a cornerstone from which the rest of the foundation should grow, missing from their relationship. Lauren knew she could deny reading the coded materials on the USB drive until she ran out of breath, and Chris wouldn't believe her any more than he did about not contacting Ryan or knowing where he had gone.

She didn't know where he had gone. A few places came to mind, but how he could have reached those locations without a vehicle and if he truly was wounded, she couldn't figure out.

Her conscience told her she should give Chris the list of places where he might find Ryan—his mother's house, the summer cottages of a few friends. Then Chris could arrest her brother and walk out of her life. That course of action was best for both of them.

But not for Ryan. Ryan had fled custody for a reason. *Not because you're guilty, please.* Thinking the words was as useless as saying them. Of course he was guilty of something. Why else would he have those files so encrypted an expert was needed to decode them once she, another sort of expert, had got into them?

"I thought Ryan sold real estate." Chris leaned his hips on the desk as though planning a long chat. "What would he be doing with a password-protected file in code?"

So Chris was reading her mind.

"I don't know."

She had asked herself the same question a dozen times while working to break the passwords.

"Do you still believe he's innocent of everything he's been accused of?" Chris persisted.

"He's guilty of assaulting a courtroom guard and fleeing custody."

That inconvenient fact she could not get out of her head—did an innocent man need to flee?

"Why would he run if he's innocent?" Chris spoke her fearful query aloud.

Lauren stood to place distance between herself and Chris and glanced around to see if anyone was listening to their conversation.

Sheriff Davis sat behind his desk talking on the phone and rubbing two fingers on his temple as though he suffered from a headache. The other men on duty had taken up positions in the break room, either watching a twenty-four-hour news station, or sitting at a table where two computers had been set up. The three men were so studiously appearing to not listen to Lauren and Chris's conversation, giving up their front desk stations, that she suspected they had and would hear every word. Lauren lowered her voice to just above a murmur.

"Maybe Ryan doesn't trust a justice system that has him convicted before he stands trial. Now, if you will excuse me, I'll go ask one of those deputies if he will take me to the lake house so I can get my car and return to Grand Rapids." She started to turn away.

"I can't let you do that," Chris said.

Lauren stopped midstep. "You can't *let* me? Who are you to let or not let me do anything?" She tried to keep her tone even, but feared her voice rose with annoyance.

In the break room doorway, Deputy Davis blushed. "Can we do anything to help you, Miss Wexler? Is that federal man bothering you?"

Chris scowled as he shoved his hands into his sweatpants pockets and shifted his weight from one foot to the other, avoiding Lauren's eyes. "Not any more than my duties demand." He lowered his voice to a level signaling his words were for Lauren's ears only. "I can't have you going straight to Ryan and helping him or warning him I'm in the area and hunting him."

"I can't go straight to Ryan if I don't know where he is."

"Look me in the eye and tell me you don't know where he is."

Lauren looked into Chris's eyes. For a moment, gazing into those lake-blue depths, she felt as though she were tumbling from a high dive, falling, falling, falling, soon to strike the icy surface of the water with a graceless smack. Or, worse, go straight to the bottom and crash on the rocks.

She blinked. Fatigue. She was just exhausted.

"I don't know where he is, Chris." She sighed. "I can think of a few places he might try to get to. But I don't know how…" Her throat closed and her eyes stung. "I saw blood on the snow. If he was wounded, I don't know how he got anywhere."

"A vehicle stashed somewhere?" Chris suggested.

Lauren nodded. "I thought of that. He got up here somehow after all. But if someone gave him a ride and dropped him off at my place, he's on his own in the woods." She looked away and caught sight of the sheriff in his office, now with his head in his hands and looking as worn as she felt. "I doubt he could have survived being out there all night."

"I'm sorry, Lauren." Chris touched her hand. "I wouldn't want anyone to die alone in the woods in the middle of winter, regardless of who they are or what they did."

Lauren nodded, unable to speak for several moments.

"As soon as a team can get here," Chris continued, "they will be combing the woods for Ryan and the men chasing him and us."

"That's a lot of ruined Christmases."

"It's our duty."

"Of course it is. Believe it or not, I understand."

"I know you do."

The air hung heavy between them, as stale as the pervasive scent of overheated coffee in the tiny sheriff's department. She had always known what would be his duty once he chose to become a deputy US marshal. Apprehending federal prisoners was one of those duties.

She glanced toward the sheriff. "He doesn't mind you all taking over his territory?"

"With a department this size?" Chris shook his head.

"So you'll be joining the hunt yourself, I presume?" Lauren glanced at his shoes. "Provided you have more appropriate clothes to wear?"

"I do have more appropriate clothes in the Jeep, but I won't be joining the hunt through the woods."

Lauren stiffened. "Why not?"

"I don't want you to be on your own, especially not at your house," Chris explained. "Those men aren't going to give up on hunting us down."

Lauren's head snapped up. "But they know we're

here. If they are after the USB drive, they must know we would turn it in for safekeeping here."

"Sure, they'll figure that out. But they could be afraid we know what it contains. Or they may believe you know where Ryan is."

"In other words, I'm not safe on my own, even a hundred miles away."

Despite the warmth radiating from the space heater below the desk, Lauren might as well have been back outside with nothing for warmth other than an ancient afghan. Cold seeped clear to her marrow.

"I'd like to say otherwise, but I can't." Chris rubbed his arms as though he too experienced the chill.

"Then what do I do? I have no clothes other than these. I have no money or credit cards or even ID. I don't even have my license. And we can't forget my cell phone is still sitting on the counter." She sighed. "At least it was. If I could just get inside to pick up a few things…"

"I think we can do that when the sun comes up," Chris said. "With the snowfall, we should be able to see if anyone has been near there since the deputies looked around."

"And then what?" Lauren wanted to sag with relief at the idea of gathering her possessions around her.

Her things—her house and car, the books, games and mementos of travel she'd collected—were all she found solid and dependable in her life. Every person left. Pets didn't live long enough. But things waited for her return to the lake. The pages of old mysteries opened beneath her fingers to well-read passages and the sweet mustiness of ancient paper and ink. Familiar. Friendly. Comforting.

"Then what?" Chris stared past Lauren's shoulder, his eyes out of focus. "You'll take me to the nearest location you think we'll find Ryan."

Lauren shook her head. "I don't think he'll go there. It's just a thought."

"Any thoughts are good at this point," Chris said.

"It's a relative of his, so I don't think he's likely to go there."

Chris gave her a skeptical glance, then looked away again. "He went to you."

"He was desperate."

"He's still desperate, Lauren."

"I suppose he is." Lauren shoved her fingers into her hair, wincing at its tangled mess and the thought of how bad she must look. "I'll tell you, but I won't go there with you."

"Why not? Is it unsafe?" Chris's tone was hard.

"It's not dangerous." Lauren's shoulders twitched to turn and see what Chris looked at instead of her. "But it's someplace I don't want to go."

"Why?"

"Because—" Lauren sighed. "Because it's his mother's house."

Chris looked blank. "His mother's still alive? I thought—I forgot—"

"That my father had three wives walk out on him?" She twisted her lips in an artificial smile. "The difference between Ryan's mother and mine is that Ryan's didn't walk out on him too."

Her mother leaving her behind still hurt.

Lauren swallowed the sadness from abandonment to the recesses of her soul, then continued, "Our father got custody before he went to prison. After he was arrested, Donna took Ryan in, and my grandmother got me."

"So why don't you want to go there?" Chris asked.

Lauren shrugged. "She doesn't like me."

An understatement if ever there was one.

She started to remind him of the one time he'd met Ryan's mother, but the phone rang beside her, and her hand reached in the reflexive impulse to answer. Chris reacted the same, and their hands collided above the instrument, his covering hers, warm, strong, a little calloused, hers cold but warming in an instant beneath his touch—warmth that spread up her arm to her face.

She snatched her hand free and backed up a step. Her foot connected with the desk chair, sending it wheeling across the floor to smack against a filing cabinet with a metallic clang.

"Blackwell?" Sheriff Davis called from his office. "It's for you. Line one."

Chris's need to pick up the receiver for real this time and push the button for the correct line gave Lauren time to recover from her clumsiness, from her mortification. She crossed the floor to retrieve the chair, but Deputy Davis was already there, pushing the errant seat toward her.

"Maybe you should sit down, Miss Wexler." He grinned at her. "You look tired."

"I am." She eyed the chair, drawn to the idea of sinking into its worn vinyl seat.

She shook her head. "If I sit down, I may not want to get up."

"I know what you mean." The deputy blushed. "I get off duty in fourteen minutes and then I'm all for my bed. After I eat breakfast."

"I hope you make yourself a good one."

Carrying on a mundane conversation with the young man kept her from eavesdropping on Chris's conversation. Still, a few words seeped through, including "Donna Delaney."

"I can get there faster..." Then, finally, "I don't know... Thanks. That's too easy."

Lauren gave up trying not to listen and faced Chris.

"She needs some things from her house first..." Chris said to the person on the other end of the phone line. "Thanks. I can be there in less than an hour." He replaced the handset into the cradle and faced Lauren. "Let's go."

"Want us to give you an escort?" Sheriff Davis asked. "If you can wait a few minutes, I'll go with you on my way home."

For some sleep, Lauren hoped for his sake.

"Thanks. Backup would be nice if we have trouble." Chris nodded to Davis. "We can afford a few minutes."

"Give me time to write some instructions for the head deputy coming on duty at seven. Five minutes?" Davis rubbed his eyes and yawned, looking like a sleepy child despite his size. "I've been here since seven o'clock yesterday morning."

No wonder the man looked so exhausted. Then again, Lauren had been awake for almost as long, nearly an entire day. No wonder she felt so exhausted. She had closed her eyes when washing up in the bathroom, not wanting to see how awful her appearance was.

"I'll be out in five." Sheriff Davis retreated to his office.

Lauren ducked into the ladies' room to avoid Chris. She still wouldn't look at herself in the mirror. She needed a hairbrush and a toothbrush, and some lipstick wouldn't ago amiss.

Vanity. Chris didn't care what she looked like. Not now. Once he thought—or at least said—she was beautiful.

Enough time wasted in the ladies' room, Lauren exited as Davis returned with a puffy jacket that gave Lauren a stab of envy over how warm it would be in the cold December air.

Soon she would have her own jacket, her gloves, her boots with the fleece lining so warm she could wear them without socks most of the time. Her toes tingled in anticipation.

She wrapped herself in the blanket Deputy Davis had lent her, figuring she could give it back at her house, then called goodbyes and thank-yous to the deputies and headed for the door.

"Wait." Chris slipped his hand beneath her elbow. "Let me go first to make sure no one is in the parking lot who shouldn't be there."

Of course. Those men could be lurking with their snowmobile and guns.

Lauren nodded and waited for Chris and the sheriff to exit the building first.

The door opened on a blast of frigid wind. No more snow fell. The sky had cleared, promising a brilliant sunrise in an hour. That meant colder weather.

Did you find shelter, Ryan?

She doubted they would find him at his mother's. Once his actions had endangered Lauren, he wouldn't do the same to Donna. He would steer clear of those he knew. But where? Though she knew she would have to tell Chris if she thought of other locations or be accused of—and even prosecuted for—obstruction of justice, or something like that, Lauren wanted to know where her brother had gone to hide, to find warmth and protection. She held no faith that US marshals, unless they had access to search-and-rescue dogs, could find Ryan in the north woods. Maybe if they gathered a host of local law enforcement. She didn't think so though. Ryan and she had grown up around there until Lauren's mother left and their father wanted a change of scenery, a migration south.

Of course he went south to be near the border and the coast. It made his activities easier.

Criminal activities.

Chris waved to her from his SUV and she stepped into the parking lot.

"Wait," he called. "I'll come to you."

Seeing the glaze of black ice shining in the lights, she was happy to wait, hugging the rough blanket closer. Across from her, Chris started his vehicle and the sheriff did the same to his. Headlights arced across the ice and piled snow as Chris pulled from his space and turned the Jeep so the passenger-side door would face Lauren. In the moments it took him to reach her, she began a list of what she needed from her house. Her cell phone and laptop, for sure. Boots, coat, gloves, most definitely. Comfortable clothes like jeans and sweaters, pajamas and slippers. She would grab a few books too. She didn't know when she would be able to return. Probably not until Ryan was caught. And certainly not until the men who had chased her and Chris were caught.

The SUV pulled up beside her and Chris leaned across to open the door. She climbed in and yanked the door closed.

"Fasten your seat belt," Chris said.

"Yes, Mom."

He waited for her to click the buckle, then headed out of the lot and onto the road. The sky was still dark this time of year this far north. Chris drove with concentration. Though the road had been plowed, patches of ice were always a hazard. Even the best drivers could spin out on black ice if they drove too fast.

But the silence in the Jeep was uncomfortably dense. Lauren squirmed in her seat. She adjusted, then readjusted, the heater vents in front of her. She wished Chris would turn on the radio for a news or weather report, then thought how her brother might be in that news and was glad the radio remained off.

The silence, save for the roar of the powerful engine and whoosh of wind whipping past the windows, grew too uncomfortable within the first mile and a half.

"So did you get permission to babysit me?" Lauren blurted.

"If you want to call it that. You're a witness. Part of my job is to protect witnesses."

Lauren knew that. When he'd told her he was applying to become a deputy US marshal, she had looked up their duties—and known Chris and she had no future.

And maybe that was for the best. He had made a major decision without talking to her about it first. He had announced his decision; he hadn't asked her opinion about it.

Because he knew she would say no way?

That hurt still. She hadn't known it did until he'd collapsed on her deck the previous night.

She drew in a deep breath to ease the tightness around her ribs—

"I smell smoke."

Chris sniffed. "It's cold out. Everyone around here uses wood-burning stoves or fireplaces."

"It's too strong for that." The tightness in her middle turned to nausea. She wanted to demand Chris drive faster but didn't dare. He might, which wasn't safe.

Ahead of them, she saw Davis lower his window, then lean forward as though talking. A radio? He must smell the smoke, as well. He must know this was too heavy, too intense.

No, no, no, it wasn't what she feared. Fires happened to other people. She was too careful.

"How far?" She could barely squeeze out the two words through a constricted throat.

"A mile."

A mile and the smoke was worse. Half a mile and they could see it against the lightening sky.

"I'm going to be sick." Lauren spoke the words so softly Chris must not have heard her, for he kept driving. A quarter mile. Two hundred yards. A hundred.

Davis pulled over to the side of the road where the monstrous truck had waited to pounce on them the night before. He lowered his window again to wave them over.

"Don't stop," Lauren cried. "I have to see."

"I don't think it's a good idea," Chris said.

He drove past the end of her driveway. Despite its length, that was close enough for Lauren to catch a glimpse of orange fire blazing against the still-blackened western horizon at the far end of the tree-lined lane.

Lauren's cry filled the cabin of the Jeep like an explosion. Before Chris realized what she intended, she had released the buckle on her seat belt and flung open the door.

"Don't—" Chris spoke to empty air.

Lauren plowed through the layer of new-fallen snow on her driveway, arms out for balance, legs pumping.

Chris flung himself from his seat and raced after her. "Lauren, wait."

Though his voice rang loudly enough to be heard above the roar of the fire, she seemed not to hear him. The blanket slipped from her shoulders, and still she continued toward the fire.

"Is she nuts?" Davis joined Chris in pursuit, gaining ground with his booted feet. "Miss Wexler, stop. There could be someone—"

The drive was pristine. Not so much as a paw print marred the smooth white surface in the shelter from wind with woods on either side.

"Miss Wexler," Davis tried again.

"Lauren, stop." Chris didn't know how she managed to move so fast in moccasins. He slipped and slid and nearly lost his balance despite his treaded boots.

Davis reached her first. "Stop." He grasped her upper arm.

She turned on him, fist raised, then realized who held her and let her arm fall. "I have to get there. It's my house. My beautiful, private—"

From a dozen feet away, Chris caught the sob in her breaking voice. His heart twisted. She loved that house. It was the closest thing she possessed to a connection to her mother, having inherited it from her grandmother. She had spent every summer of her life there.

Chris caught up with Lauren and the sheriff. He had to employ all his willpower not to wrap his arms around her and hold her close. She needed comforting, yet he no longer had a right to give her that human contact, that shoulder to cry on.

"I'm sorry." Those words were inadequate and all Chris could think to say.

Lauren raised her head, and tears flowed down her face. "I suppose you think I deserve this."

Chris flinched as though her raised fist of a moment ago had reached its mark in his gut. "Do you really think that little of me you'd believe I would wish this on anyone, especially you?"

"I'm sorry. That wasn't fair. I—I'm... Why would anyone do this to me?" She glanced from Chris to Davis and back to Chris.

"To hide any evidence they might have left behind," Chris said. "Our guys couldn't get here any quicker."

"We got those two bullets out of some woodwork," Davis said, "but that's all we were equipped to handle."

"At least there's that." Chris looked to the road at the sound of sirens. "Fire?"

"It's a volunteer force, but they're pretty efficient." Davis headed back toward his SUV. "We need to get out of their way."

"Why bother with a fire truck?" Lauren wiped her hands on her face. "There's nothing left to save."

"They need to make sure it doesn't spread to the woods," Davis said.

"Of course they do." Lauren started to follow Davis toward the road.

Chris fell into step beside her. "I wish I could have stopped this from happening, Lauren."

"Thank you." She kept her face turned away from him.

"Me saying sorry doesn't help, does it?"

She didn't respond.

"Let's get you back into the Jeep and warm."

He wanted to get her away altogether. Who knew if the men lurked in the trees or not. He needed to call his office. They would have to send a different kind of team, an arson team.

The Jeep was still running, doors open, heat spilling into the morning. Not looking at him, Lauren climbed into the passenger seat and pulled the door closed. Chris rounded the vehicle and grabbed his phone from the console, then closed the driver's-side door. He thought Lauren might protest him shutting her into the vehicle and making a call out of her hearing, but she sat with her head down and her hands over her face.

His chest, his arms, his being ached to hold her, to remind her those were just things, that memories were what mattered, what lasted.

If he let himself, he could conjure up a hundred or more memories of visiting that house, visiting her after they met on the lakeshore, where his parents had owned a summer cottage before his father's death. Barbecuing on sultry summer nights, reading together or playing board games on cold rainy days. His mom and sister had always been there, discreet chaperones. Sometimes his dad had been able to join them and the games had grown livelier, the gatherings boisterous.

The fire trucks screamed past him. Once they reached the house and the morning grew quiet enough for Chris to hear himself think, he made his call. Then he joined the sheriff. He and Lauren needed to be going, but Chris doubted ten minutes for her to grieve alone wouldn't make much difference, and talking with Davis was preferable to Chris's own painful memories.

"Is she all right?" Davis asked.

Chris refrained from snapping, "What do you think?" and instead shook his head. "This place was special to her."

"I thought you two knew each other before last night." Davis arched one brow.

"Just a little. We were going to get married five years ago."

"I wasn't expecting that one." Davis looked like he wanted to say more, but was too polite to ask.

"My father was killed in the line of duty and I changed my career to the Marshals Service. End of engagement. End of story."

"Some people can't take the stress of their spouse being in danger." Davis peered down the driveway. "If those men after you two went this far, they must know their DNA is in the system."

"It's gone now." Chris glanced toward the Jeep. "I should get going. I need to check out every lead on the escaped prisoner's whereabouts I can."

"I'll keep you informed on what we find here." Davis scrubbed his hands over his face. "Usually the worst thing that goes down here is drunken teenagers causing trouble."

"This isn't in my usual day's work either." Chris shook hands with the sheriff, then jogged back to the Jeep.

Lauren didn't so much as glance his way when he swung into his seat and released the parking brake.

"Where does Ryan's mother live?" he asked.

"You got the address from your office, didn't you?" Her voice was muffled behind her hands.

"I have an address. You can tell me how to get there."

For a response, she picked up his cell phone. "Unlock your phone and I'll put it into your map app."

"GPS is terrible here." Despite his claim, Chris held out his hand to unlock his phone with his fingerprint.

Lauren located a GPS map and inputted the address. From the corner of his eye, he noted it was the right one. Not that he expected her to lead him astray.

Which was a little odd. He should have expected her to misdirect him given the opportunity. Then again, he had taken ten minutes to realize she could drive off with his Jeep.

Fatigue or growing trust? He wasn't ready to surrender to the former and still doubted the latter was possible.

"Drive south fifteen miles," the bland female voice directed from his phone's speaker.

Chris drove south with the sky turning rosy to his left, still dark to his right. Trees lined both sides of the road, broken occasionally by roads branching in other directions or driveways leading to houses and farms and the occasional campground by a lake. Traffic remained light with just a few vehicles, SUVs mostly, passing Chris going in the opposite direction or turning from one of the side roads.

All the while, Lauren said nothing. She had stopped crying for the most part. With her head against the headrest and her eyes closed, a sporadic tear rolled down her cheek, catching the glow of the rising sun, the flash of a headlight still on. Chris sought for the right words to say to comfort her, to give her hope. Nothing came to him but senseless clichés: *It was just wood and glass. Things are replaceable. Thank the Lord you weren't inside.*

She knew that. To her, however, the house was more than wood and glass. It was something she had possessed too little of in her life—security, stability, family history she wasn't ashamed of.

Appropriate words failing Chris, he thought up any words, ordinary small talk, anything to break the silence.

"Lots of people will be glad of a white Christmas." He tossed out the first volley.

She remained unresponsive for so long he thought she was going to maintain her stillness. Then she raised her head and opened her eyes, the irises golden with their sheen of tears. "The snow is pretty."

"Do you still cross-country ski?"

"I do."

"I didn't see any skis in the garage."

"I left them in Grand Rapids. I was alone this trip and don't like to ski by myself when this area is so empty this time of year."

"Smart."

With whom did she ski the other times?

He couldn't ask. It was none of his business. But the pang of envy for her skiing partner took him by surprise.

Had she found someone else? He wouldn't be surprised. She was smart and pretty and had always been great company.

"Do you ski with a group?" He couldn't stop himself from asking.

"Your turn's coming up in another half mile."

"In one half mile," the computer voice said from his phone, "turn left onto Pine Ridge Road."

Chris laughed. "Pine Ridge? A ridge in the lower peninsula?"

She managed a half smile. "It's a fancy subdivision. For some reason, developers like names like that. It makes it sound as if you'll get some mountain-vista-type view."

"Some water and trees would suit me fine for a view," Chris said. "And that should be easy to come by up here."

"It is." Her smile flickered and died.

If he hadn't been driving, Chris would have kicked himself. Her house had stood with a view of water and trees—had stood there for fifty years or more.

Glad of the diversion, he slowed, flicking on his turn signal to exit from the two-lane highway to the subdivision road. Other vehicles slowed behind him, headlights off in the brightening morning, harder to see against a backdrop of trees and snow. Oncoming traffic whooshed past, one car, two, then an opening wide enough for him to slip through and make the turn.

The new road wound through trees so uniform in size and distance from one another, they couldn't be from a natural forest, but planted. Then the view opened to a lake surrounded with houses so similar they appeared more like game pieces set on a board than dwellings for individuals.

"How do you figure out which house is the right one?" Chris asked.

"I'll recognize Donna's house." Lauren peered through the windshield toward the houses on the left. "It faces the lake. She's a successful Realtor and she also got a great settlement from my father, apparently."

"She must have. These houses can't be cheap." Chris

scanned the houses for numbers. "Her house number is four-forty-one."

"The numbers are above the garage doors in script. I remember that, and I remember if you pass your house, you have to drive all the way around the lake because they made this road too narrow to turn around, so it's one-way."

"And the residents put up with it?"

"For a view of the water? People put up with a lot for that."

"It's a man-made pond."

"It's big enough for small motor craft and fishing and—I think someone wants to pass us." She had her head tilted so she could look at the rearview mirror.

Chris glanced in the mirror too. Sure enough, a gray sedan rode their bumper. "Not very bright with these patches of ice on the road."

Nonetheless, he pulled off to the side to let the sedan pass. The driver floored the pedal as though the pavement were dry and the road a straightaway on a racetrack. In moments, the dull-colored vehicle vanished around a curve. Chris half expected to hear squealing tires and a crash. But the morning remained quiet and calm in the community, as he pulled back onto the road. Few people were out that early other than an old man in a robe, pajamas and slippers retrieving his newspaper from the front stoop to the right, and a girl of no more than ten or so walking an Irish wolfhound nearly as big as she was on the left. Chris braked to let her cross the road and head for the beach, where snow covered the sand.

"How far to Donna Delaney's?" Chris asked.

"Around the curve where that sedan turned. Not far."

An odd sensation of anticipation tensing in his gut, Chris took the curve at a more sedate pace than had the sedan. He didn't want to pass Mrs. Delaney's house, and instinct told him to keep a lookout for unusual activity.

Like someone running across the frozen waters of the lake.

"Chris!" Lauren cried the same instant he spotted the figure setting out from the edge of the lake—not running, but skating.

Chris slowed. "Who do you think it is?"

Lauren pointed at the lake, her face as white as the snow. "I think—I think it's Ryan."

EIGHT

Before Chris could hit the brake, Lauren had the door open and was running across the road.

"Stop," he called after her.

Ignoring him, she darted between two houses along a—thankfully—shoveled sidewalk, until she reached the beach. A fairly shallow man-made expanse of water, the lake appeared frozen solid. The skating man must have known it would be. Experience of a resident, or did she recognize the way her brother skated, smoothly, effortlessly? The brother, who had taught her to skate, to cross-country ski, to downhill ski. Quite simply, to love winter.

Maybe it wasn't him. Maybe it was a resident who liked to skate to get his morning exercise when the weather made running impossible. Ryan had been wounded after all, hadn't he? This man didn't seem to move like he was injured. Besides, how had he got this far without a car?

Because he had one. That gray sedan. Someone had picked him up. An accomplice? A kindhearted and probably foolish motorist giving a ride to a hitchhiker?

No matter. She had to know the truth even if she made a fool of herself getting there.

"Lauren, stop." Chris was gaining on her. In boots, he was better equipped for running in the snow than she was in her moccasins.

She might as well have been trying to run in sand. Snow filled her shoes and weighed down her feet. With one step she landed knee-deep in a drift, and with the next, her foot slid on ice under the top powder.

Chris's hand beneath her elbow prevented her from falling. "You can't go after him, Lauren."

"I can't catch him." She sank to her knees in the snow.

Chris took off across the ice in pursuit of the skater. Chris wore winter boots, not good for running—especially on ice—yet he seemed to be gaining on the skater. Conscious of her jeans growing wet as her body heat melted the snow beneath, Lauren watched the two men who had meant the most to her in her life.

They were still a good fifty feet apart, Ryan not quite as fast as she thought he should be able to go on skates, Chris faster than she expected for someone in snow boots on ice. Chris shouted, too far away for Lauren to catch the words. She guessed what they were: "Stop! Deputy US Marshal," or something of the sort.

Ryan merely set his runners shrieking over the ice.

And now his limp was obvious, one leg dragging just a little behind the other with each gliding swoosh of a stride forward. It slowed him. Lauren knew he could skate so much faster than this, and he was lagging.

But not enough for Chris to catch him. The gap grew to a hundred feet, a hundred fifty. And then an island in the lake with some trees growing from it blocked the men from view. Lauren rose, brushing snow from her jeans, and turned toward Donna's house. She wasn't sure if she could do anything for Ryan or Chris other than pray for their safety, pray Ryan would be smart and let himself get caught, pray that Chris did nothing stupid.

She didn't need to worry about that. Chris Blackwell didn't do stupid things, except maybe fall in love with the daughter of a criminal. He'd said he didn't care. Her father lived far away and had nothing to do with their lives. She had changed her name so it wouldn't be the same as her parents'.

Then Chris's father was murdered by a sniper while transporting a prisoner, who had then escaped. Chris changed careers, and Lauren came to her senses.

Twice since she broke her engagement, Lauren's father had come under suspicion. Each time, a grand jury failed to return an indictment for lack of evidence. When Ryan had been arrested, their father assured him he would go free, as well. But the prosecutor was convinced he had enough evidence for an indictment.

And Ryan had run, making himself appear guilty to the public. The escape would probably firm up the prosecutor's case in the eyes of the jury. How could Lauren believe her brother was innocent now? He kept running from the law.

Why had Ryan tried to get to his mother? Donna surely wouldn't give him shelter. She knew better than that. She knew her house was one place the law would seek her son. Yet there he was, flying across the lake and away from Chris.

Ears straining for any sounds off the lake, beginning to shiver from her wet pants and shoes, Lauren headed for Donna's house. Steps led from the beach to a hedge-trimmed lawn bisected with a walkway straight to the deck. The walkway was already shoveled. Paw prints in the snow suggested why—Donna had a dog she needed to walk. A dog! She had, according to Ryan, ignored his pleas for a pet when he was young. Yet the telltale signs of a canine ranged across the snow. Not a small purse-sized dog judging from the indentations, but something substantial.

And dangerous?

Lauren mounted the steps from the beach to the lawn. A woof like a roll of thunder reverberated from the house. Lauren paused at the top step. "You can't be all that dangerous," she said aloud to convince herself. "Surely the homeowners' association here wouldn't allow a vicious dog."

She continued up the walk and climbed a second set of steps in order to reach the deck. No more barks. That was promising. He—or she—had given a warning and settled to wait for the visitor.

Lauren turned toward the lake at the top of the deck steps. Higher up, she might be able to see more of the action on the lake.

She did—Chris returning. He stalked across the ice with his hands thrust into the pockets of his coat, his head down. He might have simply been protecting his face from the cold by tucking his chin into the collar of his coat. Or he might be a man defeated, thwarted yet again. Lauren suspected the latter. Those were the controlled strides of a frustrated or maybe an angry man.

She decided to wait for him. "Coward," she muttered to herself.

She didn't want to face Donna and the dog on her own.

Then, behind her, the door opened. "Saber, sit." The voice was deep and rough like that of someone who had smoked too many cigarettes. Indeed, the stench of stale tobacco smoke rolled into the pristine morning air.

Lauren recognized the voice and the smell. They belonged to Ryan's mother, Donna Delaney, her father's first wife with a razor blade for a tongue, and now a dog named Saber for a companion.

Slowly, Lauren faced the woman she hadn't seen in three years or more—and her canine. Her black Labrador had a pink rhinestone collar and huge doggy grin, tongue lolling from one side, big brown eyes shining with gentleness and a tail that wagged so hard it seemed to stop her from sitting as commanded.

"Saber?" Lauren laughed. "More like a sweetheart."

"I wanted a pit bull, but the homeowners' association doesn't allow them." Donna frowned at the dog, but her hand stroking the glossy black head spoke another message.

Donna had once been a beautiful woman, with a smooth, olive complexion and thick, dark hair. Now two lines like an eleven marred her forehead between her eyebrows. Too much makeup, even that early in the morning, disguised the true color of her skin—skin too unlined not to have been treated with surgery or Botox at the least. And her hair was a startling ash-blond in comparison to her deep brown eyes.

She raised those eyes from the dog to Lauren. "So, Lauren Wexler, what has the cat's daughter dragged in?"

"My mother was not—" Lauren clamped her teeth shut on the reflexive defense of her mother.

Her mother didn't deserve defense. She had taken another woman's husband. She had abandoned him and her child. Lauren could forgive her with the grace of God, and she wanted to find excuses for her, yet in the end, her mother was responsible for her own defense, as she was responsible for her own actions.

"I'm here with Deputy US Marshal Christopher Blackwell," Lauren said instead.

His footfalls crunched on the brick steps to the deck. "Good morning, ma'am. I am here on official business."

"I watch the news. But if you're looking for my son," Donna said, "he isn't here. I haven't seen him."

"He just skated across the lake." Chris joined Lauren on the deck.

Donna shrugged.

The dog pawed at the door, bouncing up and down as though wanting to get to Chris to maul him with love, surely not murderous intent.

Lauren smiled at the silly creature, though something ached in her heart.

"Did you give him those skates, a vehicle to drive away in, any other kind of assistance?" Chris fired the possibilities at Donna.

"It's morning. I haven't seen or talked to anyone." Donna started to close the storm door.

She hadn't answered any of Chris's questions.

"There wasn't enough time for her to do anything," Lauren pointed out.

"She could have met him outside if she knew he was coming," Chris said.

"I haven't left the house," Donna said.

"Did you walk the dog?" Lauren asked.

Donna pointed to a hook beside the door. "She goes out on a chain."

"May we come in and talk to you?" Chris asked.

"No officer of the law is coming inside my house without a warrant." Donna closed the door further, nudging the dog out of the way.

Lauren lunged forward and grasped the handle to the screen door. "May I use your bathroom, please? And do you have a comb and an extra toothbrush? I have nothing." She didn't need to fake the tears in her eyes. "My house burned down."

"The lake house?" Donna's voice, if not her artificially smooth face, shimmered with shock. "That's terrible. Were you careless with the woodstove?"

"No, some men did it because they thought I had Ryan."

Donna's hand slipped from the door handle. The door swung back. "Maybe you better tell me what you're talking about."

"I can wait in the Jeep," Chris offered.

"You can come into the kitchen. Saber, don't—"

She issued the feeble command too late. The instant Lauren stepped over the threshold, the Labrador flung herself into her arms, licking any skin she could find, wagging from ears to the tip of her flat tail.

Lauren hugged her and laughed, then her arms were empty as the dog turned her affections on Chris.

"Great guard dog," he said with a laugh in his voice.

"She must think you're not a threat." Donna strode into a kitchen large enough for a small table and chairs tucked into an alcove overlooking the lake. "Sit here. I have coffee, but nothing to eat."

Lauren believed that. Donna was rail thin.

"Bathroom's that way." Donna pointed down a hallway. "Extra toothbrush in the vanity. What kind of coffee do you want, Mr. Deputy US Marshal? French roast,

French vanilla…" She opened a cabinet full of boxes of coffee pods for a single-serve coffee maker.

Lauren scuttled out of the room, figuring she had about five minutes before Donna got suspicious. Fortunately, the house was a small ranch-style with two bedrooms and two baths, a dining room and living room. The dining room looked barely used, its formal furniture free of ornaments, china stacked behind glass doors of the cabinet. The living room appeared almost as untouched, other than a grimy ashtray on a side table and a paperback novel facedown on the sofa. The master bedroom, however, was a mess of lived-in chaos with clothes draped over a chair, the TV on an all-news station with the sound turned down and shoes from spike heels to ballet flats scattered from one end to the other. Nothing in the room suggested Ryan had been there.

Lauren entered the guest bath, located a toothbrush and comb and set to work making herself feel slightly less scruffy, though her clothes were hopeless.

But they were the only clothes she owned outside her home in Grand Rapids, where Chris wouldn't allow her to go yet.

Her looks didn't matter. Chris cared only about her safety because letting her get hurt would make him appear rather incompetent, and Ryan might try to contact her again. How he would do that Lauren didn't know, but twenty-four hours ago, she had no idea her life would turn upside down as it had. Anything was possible.

Even, possibly, Donna setting the skates outside for Ryan without looking at him so she could claim she hadn't seen him. But why would either of them bother?

Lauren studied the sink and tub for signs of recent

use. They were spotless. Not so much as a dog hair marred their porcelain perfection. Likewise, the guest bedroom appeared to have been unused except for a rumple in the center of the bedspread to which several short black hairs clung.

Ryan's hair was chestnut like Lauren's. Like their father's.

She started to exit and return to the kitchen, then caught sight of the closet door. It wasn't open. Nor was it fully latched.

Feet silent on the thick carpet, Lauren reached the closet in half a dozen steps. She started to grasp the handle, then slipped her hand up her sleeve before turning the knob. It held men's clothes. It wasn't surprising Ryan would leave things here as he did at Lauren's house. No way to tell what might be missing. The floor was empty, where maybe shoes had stood earlier. The shelf, however, contained a backpack, a shoebox with receipts poking from beneath the lid and—

A case for ice skates.

Heart thudding slowly and sickeningly hard in her middle, Lauren drew the case from the shelf and popped up the lid. It was empty.

"Lauren, what's taking you so long?" Donna demanded from the kitchen.

Lauren wiped her eyes on her sleeve. No sense in crying. She knew Ryan had been here. She had seen him.

She started to close the case, but stopped, her eye catching a bulge on the inside of the lid. A pocket. No doubt it held blade treatment materials. She didn't need to look. Looking might help Chris catch Ryan if the pocket held anything else.

And shouldn't she do that? Help the law catch her criminal brother? Wasn't she being a criminal by not doing what she could to apprehend her brother?

She looked inside the pocket. It held a flat can of waterproofing, soft cloths, some kind of oil—

And a USB drive.

Lauren grabbed a tissue from a box on the bedside table, removed the USB drive and slid it into her pocket just as Donna knocked on the bathroom door.

With as much haste and stealth as she could, Lauren shoved the case onto the shelf, pushed the closet door to without latching it and raced across the room to the bathroom. Snatching up the comb with one hand, she opened the door with the other. "My hair took longer to detangle than I thought it would."

"Uh-huh. Well, your coffee's getting cold." Donna turned and trotted toward the kitchen, her high-heeled mules slapping the bottoms of her feet with a snap on each step.

Lauren followed. Her clothes wet once again, she was cold. Hot coffee helped. She sipped while Chris told Donna what had happened since the night before.

Donna listened, her face impassive, giving nothing away.

"Did you put the skates outside for him?" Lauren asked.

"I don't have to answer that." Donna reached for the coffee carafe. "More?"

Lauren was tempted by the warmth and the comfort of remaining in Donna's house, but she needed something to wear. Donna's clothes would never do. She was ten pounds lighter and four inches taller than Lauren.

"I need something to wear beside these clothes." Lauren met Chris's gaze. "That means I need to go home."

"We can buy something if there's a store nearby." Chris arched one brow.

Lauren nodded. "Then let's get going." Lauren turned toward the door. "Thank you for your hospitality, Donna."

Donna merely grunted and lit a cigarette.

Saber followed them to the door, her head pressed against Chris's leg.

He bent and scratched her behind one floppy ear. "You take care of your mom, okay?"

Saber wagged her tail.

Chris held the door for Lauren. Saber looked as though she might follow them, but Donna called her and she raced back to the kitchen. Lauren left the deck and began to circle the house toward the Jeep.

"Wait." Chris moved ahead of her. "Let me make sure everything's all right."

"You think Donna's in danger, don't you?" Lauren dogged Chris's heels.

"I told her to get out of here. I hope she listens."

"Unless those men have found Ryan first."

"There is that." Chris peered around the garage, then activated the remote key for the Jeep. It started with a roar. "Let's find a store where we can find you some warmer clothes and a burner phone."

"All right, but—"

"Wait until we're in the Jeep." Chris opened her door, then skirted the vehicle to climb into the driver's seat. Once they were both inside and pulling out of the subdivision, he continued, "I called the nearest marshal's office and told them where we saw Ryan and to keep an eye on his mother."

"She needs to get out of there." Lauren snapped on her seat belt, glad of the remote ignition to begin warming up the vehicle before they got in.

"I hope she does, for the sake of that dog, if nothing else."

Lauren flashed him a grin. "She fell for you in a big way."

"Dogs like me."

Females liked him. Donna had even been cordial.

Suddenly, Lauren had the impulse to ask Chris if he had a girlfriend. She opened her mouth, the query on her tongue, then shook her head. It wasn't any of her business.

She didn't want to know.

"What did you want to tell me?" Chris changed the subject back to what was important, what was her business at present, and all without realizing he was doing so.

"I found a USB drive in Donna's guest room." She fished it from her pocket, still wrapped in the protective tissue, and tossed it into the nearest cup holder. "It was in an empty ice skate case. I mean, empty of skates, that is."

"I figured she was lying about not seeing him." Chris pushed the fingers of one hand through his hair, making the waves pop up into curls around the bandage on his scalp.

Lauren clasped her hands to stop herself from reaching over and smoothing the curls down again, rather than to ensure the lump on his head had not grown larger and the wound was healing well. He had the thickest, softest hair. She loved to touch it, make it curl, then flatten it down as much as she could.

Emptiness yawned inside her. She had tried to fill it with work, with making money and buying things over the past five years. None of that had worked. And now she had lost the bulk of her most valued possessions.

"The USB drive could be nothing," Chris said, "or it could be another copy of the previous one. It might not even be his." He glanced down. "Good thinking to not touch it."

She warmed with pleasure over the compliment, which was so much like the reaction of a fourteen-year-old with a crush she wanted to hit herself in the head to get some sense back. Chris. Was. Not. For. Her. He was trying to arrest her brother. Someone would arrest her brother, who had led trouble to her. Chris could not be associated with her for that, if nothing else. She had known this for five years. Nothing had changed. If anything, things were worse.

Just as she'd predicted.

"I think I'll keep this one until we can look at it," Chris continued. "Let's find the nearest superstore." He picked up his phone, unlocked it and gave it to Lauren.

She found a store that should provide them with everything they needed. "It's twenty miles to the north."

Twenty miles more in the car with him.

After three silent miles, she turned on the radio to an all-news station.

"Nine o'clock a.m., December 24."

Christmas Eve. This was Christmas Eve, and she was stranded in an SUV with her former fiancé with nothing to say to him, while her brother was a fugitive from the

law and her father estranged because she wanted nothing
to do with someone so far from grace by his own will.

*Money is power, Lauren, my girl. Money is what
matters.* That was her father's favorite thing to say
whenever she mentioned him going to church and turning his life around.

He was wrong.

She squirmed, uneasiness settling over her.

"You need a break?" Chris asked.

Lauren shook her head. "Just thinking."

"About what?"

She hesitated before finally admitting, "My father."

"The almighty and untouchable Richard Delaney."
Chris flicked a glance her way before returning his attention to the road. "So great you won't use his name."

"Wexler is my mother's maiden name. It was my
middle name. I just dropped the Delaney."

"Why? I mean, your mother hasn't been in your life
for—how long?"

"Fifteen years." Lauren spoke to her hands clasped
on her knees. "But as far as I know, she has never done
anything illegal."

"Unlike your father?"

"Drop it, Chris. You know as well as I do that I think
my father is now a smuggler of anything he can get into
or out of the country. Just none of us has proof."

"And you wouldn't give it up if you did."

The fact he said it rather than asked it set her fingers
bunching into fists and her insides coiled tight enough
to hurt. "Of course I would. But he keeps his business
interests far out of my sight. So, how do you think your
career is going?"

"Well." Chris picked up her conversational change

without a hitch. "I travel a great deal, which I enjoy far more than being stuck behind a desk."

"At least you wouldn't get shot at behind a desk."

Chris shrugged. "Part of the job."

"So your mom and sister can lose you too?"

Lauren regretted the words the instant they were out of her mouth. They might be true, but they were an unkind reminder of his father's death at the hands of an unknown assassin.

"They're happy to have me in law enforcement."

They probably were. His mother and sister were two of the kindest people Lauren had ever met.

"Even though you're missing Christmas?"

"Maybe I won't, if we can catch Ryan by tonight."

So Ryan would spend Christmas Eve in prison. And she would spend Christmas Eve...where?

A hotel somewhere.

Once upon a time, she could have spent it with Chris's family.

Sadness left her unwilling to talk more. Chris didn't pursue further conversation, so she closed her eyes and leaned her head against the window. The sonorous voice of the newscaster lulled her into a doze. Happy, feelgood news today. No one wanted death and destruction on the holiday about love and peace on earth.

Lauren would settle for peace in her heart for the moment.

Conversation died. The road, clear of snow beneath a sunny sky, seemed to stretch forever. When they reached the discount department store, the parking lot thronged with vehicles and people on Christmas Eve, last-minute shoppers picking up gifts, wrapping paper and food. Chris pulled the Jeep into a spot about as far from the door as they could be. "Go ahead and get the clothes you need, warm stuff especially, and I'll get you a phone."

"I'll pay you back."

"Sure." Chris slammed his door and rounded the Jeep to open hers. Such courtesy had been lacking in her life—along with Chris.

"Who knows what I can find here."

"You can manage without your usual high-end stuff?"

"I meant the store will be picked over."

Chris locked the Jeep and they headed out in silence, weaving between cars and carts and baby strollers with hurrying parents pushing.

Halfway there, he paused beside a pickup truck and faced her. "I'm sorry. That was uncalled-for."

"Apology accepted." She managed a smile. "I do like a bargain, you know."

Some of her tension eased, and she entered the crowded store with intent. She needed slacks or jeans, a couple of sweaters and sturdier shoes. Though boots seemed unlikely, she managed to find a pair of ankle boots with decent treads. Items chosen, she located the backpack to carry it all. The only one left was bright orange. She shuddered, but added it to the cart, then met Chris, who was already holding a place in the check-out line.

"Do you think I can change here?" she asked him.

"The restrooms are by the door, so probably."

What she'd give for a shower.

She settled for putting on clean clothes, warmer clothes, and brushing her hair, then applying a touch of lipstick. Feeling more herself, she exited the restroom, but she didn't see Chris. He, however, must have been watching for her inside the second set of doors, as he met her in moments.

"I think it's getting colder again," he said by way of greeting.

He was right. The sun had ducked between a layer of dark clouds and the wind had increased.

"And now the car will be cold." She rubbed her arms.

The sweater and jacket she now wore surpassed the shirt and blanket she had used for warmth. Still, she shivered.

"I'll get the car started as soon as we're within range. It won't be too bad by the time we get to it."

Once again, they threaded their way through other shoppers on their way across the parking lot. The crowds and traffic seemed thinner already, people heading home to begin the celebration of the holiday. Halfway there, Chris paused to press the remote starter.

And the world exploded with a flash of light and an earth-shattering boom.

NINE

Chris wrapped his arms around Lauren and drew her to the pavement behind the rack of carts. Beyond their shelter, dozens of car alarms began to honk and shriek. People screamed, shouted, wailed while charging back into the store or around it. Through it all, one word rang in Chris's head—*bomb*.

The explosion had been a car bomb. He didn't need to look to know the vehicle had been his. Pressing the remote starter had triggered the device.

If they hadn't parked at the far end of the lot, people— children, old folks, holiday shoppers—could have been injured. Or, worse, many could have been killed. A few other cars had been parked back there, people like him wanting to be able to exit quickly. If any of those were on their way to their vehicles, in their vehicles… If he had waited longer to press the starter…

Disaster.

Chris held on to Lauren more tightly. She was shaking. He was shaking. Lauren's fingers gripped his shoulders hard enough to hurt. He welcomed the discomfort. It helped him focus, think, plan.

They should stick around and make a police report.

He should tell the local authorities the exploded vehicle was his. If they were fortunate, the sheriff's office would take Chris and Lauren to the station for questioning, to a safe place.

If they even were safe with law enforcement. Chris never liked thinking cops or other deputy US marshals were corrupt, but he knew it happened. Maybe Ryan had run because he knew of danger within law enforcement.

Even if the local sheriff's department was on the up-and-up, Chris couldn't get Lauren to them soon enough. The crowd was too dense, too panicked. By the time Chris was able to get through to officers and show his credentials and make a report, the press would have arrived. This was too juicy a story for any newsperson to pass up, even on Christmas Eve. Cars just didn't explode in discount store parking lots in small towns without some sensation lying behind it. And when the press arrived with their cameras and live feeds, Chris and Lauren's faces would be all over the news. Those who had planted the bomb would know they had been unsuccessful in killing them.

"We have to get out of here." Chris spoke into Lauren's ear, taking just a second to enjoy the softness of her hair against his face.

Lauren nodded and released her hold on him, then lifted her head to touch her lips to his ear. "Where to?"

That touch had oddly felt like a kiss, her lips surprisingly warm against his cold earlobe.

Chris shivered, momentarily forgetting the question.

"Chris?" She spoke his name, that one syllable on her tongue warming, soothing, steadying.

"Away from here for the moment. We'll decide where after that." He rose, drawing her to her feet with him.

Hand in hand, though gloves made the touch impersonal, they joined the throng reentering the store. Several employees stood inside the entry encouraging people, "Walk, don't run," like hall monitors in an elementary school. Heads down, Chris and Lauren crept past the employees, following the crowd.

It grew thinner and quieter as everyone moved deeper into the store. Chris edged them to an outside wall, seeking another exit. With one hand, he held Lauren as though he needed to keep her afloat with his grip. With the other, he fished his wallet and his credentials out of his pocket.

For a moment, guilt seized him over his intention to use his deputy US marshal credentials to leave the scene. But they couldn't stay in the vicinity. Doing so was simply unsafe for both of them.

Behind the sporting goods, they found the employees' entrance. Two men of Chris's height, but bulkier, blocked the doorway. "You can't go in there, buddy," one of them said, holding up his arms.

"We need to be outside and this is the closest exit." Chris held up his wallet.

The men exchanged a look, then stepped aside. "You got here fast."

"I was in the area." Chris nodded to the men and he and Lauren walked past, through a break room with tables and chairs and vending machines, then to a storage room nearly as cold as the outdoors. Beyond that, two more men blocked the entry to a loading dock. These men were smaller, the space they guarded wider. No one was trying to climb onto the concrete slab to enter the store. No trucks were making deliveries on Christmas

Eve. A long drive flanked by a small parking lot, probably for employees, stretched before them.

"I'll help you down." Chris released Lauren's hand long enough to jump to the ground, then he lifted her to the drive.

"Now what?" She scanned the bleak scene. "We won't get far on foot."

"I hope we don't have to. But let's get out of sight of those fellows at the door."

They skirted the side of the building, then Chris led them between two salt-encrusted pickup trucks and across a narrow access road—where a fence blocked their way.

To the left lay the highway and chaos. To the right the fence skirted the lot of another business. Chris tried to remember what that business was. He was usually more observant, was trained to be more observant. He had been distracted on the way into the department store, watching Lauren, hurting as he hadn't in years.

"It's a restaurant," Lauren said. "An all-you-can-eat buffet, I think."

Chris started to ask how in the world she knew that, but heard the shriek of a siren flying toward them along the access road. "Let's go," he said instead.

They darted between the pickup trucks again and waited for the police car to streak past. If the occupants saw Chris and Lauren, he hoped they would think they were simply getting into their vehicle. The SUV didn't stop, so he figured they were clear from being taken to where not only the sheriff's people could talk to them, but reporters and their cameras could reach them.

"We'll go around the fence in the back," Chris said once the coast was clear.

Easier said than done. Though the woods had been cut far back from the fenced lot, brush had filled in. Piled with snow, it made tough going. Not as tough as tramping through the woods in moccasins had been the night before.

Only the night before. It felt like a lifetime ago.

Fortunately, the lot wasn't large. Snow-clad to their knees, they reached the other side of the fence and another access road, another parking lot, another restaurant. This was an anonymous fast-food place with a line of cars stretching from the drive-through window to the highway, but a nearly empty parking lot. Chris and Lauren entered by the front door. He wouldn't normally eat at a place like this, but at that moment even the oil from the kitchen smelled good, and he realized they hadn't eaten for far too long.

"We should grab some food." He glanced at Lauren.

She nodded. "I shouldn't be hungry. I mean, someone just tried to—"

He touched a finger to her lips and nodded to others close enough to hear.

"But I am hungry," she finished.

They ordered coffee, juice and sandwiches and took their food to the most isolated table they could find. No one sat close enough to overhear their conversation, and they could look through the window without being too close to it. Not surprisingly, Lauren slid into the booth with her back to the wall.

After a moment's hesitation, Chris slid in beside her. "I'm sorry to do this, but I would rather be able to see the room."

And they looked like a couple who wanted to be

not merely as alone as they could be, but also close to one another.

They were close, his left side touching her right side from shoulder to knee. Once they had removed their warm coats, the contact was electric, setting Chris's nerves on edge, robbing his appetite. He began to eat anyway. He needed the fuel regardless of its quality or lack thereof.

Lauren seemed methodical in her consumption—a sip of coffee, a bite of sandwich, a swallow of juice. Repeat. Chris found himself falling into the same pattern, neither of them speaking.

On the other side of the room, a mother tried to keep three children under five from sliding off the booth seats and running around the room. She looked harried. The children's faces glowed with youthful zeal and joy beneath shocks of red hair.

An ache began in the region of Chris's heart. Had life gone differently, had his father not been killed, had Chris and Lauren not made the decisions they had, they could have children at least the age of the younger two. They hadn't talked about children yet. Maybe they should have before they discussed marriage, but somehow the subject never came up. Chris hadn't thought that far ahead.

He hadn't thought ahead on too many things, like how lonely life was on his own. He didn't even have a pet. Pets deserved to have owners who were at home more than he was.

"Do you have a dog or cat?" he asked suddenly.

Lauren started, dropping her sandwich onto the tray. "What a strange thing to ask me."

"I guess it is." Chris glanced out the window.

The drive-through line hadn't diminished, and a crowd headed for the front door of the restaurant.

"Do you?" he pressed.

"No. I travel too much." She replaced the top half of the bun but didn't pick up the sandwich. "Or I used to travel too much until the past six months when I hired more people to do that for me."

"More management, less hands-on?"

She nodded. "I still do some software development too." She took a bite of her food, chewed, swallowed, then added, "And now I'm thinking about getting a dog or maybe a cat or both. Seeing Donna with a dog made me think having one around would be nice. What about you?"

"I also travel too much and don't see that stopping anytime soon."

But the conversation did. More people entered the dining area, sitting by the windows and discussing the explosion.

"They don't know whose car it was."

"Probably drug dealers."

"Up here?"

"Those punks are everywhere."

Chris pulled out his phone and searched for the local news headlines. What people said was about as much information as the reporters had. He inspected online videos to see if he and Lauren showed up in any of them, but the screen was too small to tell.

What he did see was that his battery was running low. He hadn't given it a full charge, only increasing power in spurts when in his vehicle.

"Did you lose the phone you bought for me?" Lauren asked.

"It's in my coat pocket, but it'll need to be charged too."

They looked at one another, the message clear—where would they do that? For that matter, how would they get anywhere?

Chris handed Lauren his phone. "Will you call Mrs. Delaney? Giving us a ride will get her away from her house."

"I can't call Donna."

"I think she'll understand. It will also show her how dangerous these people are."

"But I don't know her number." Lauren crumpled the wrapping from her sandwich. "We weren't exactly friendly with one another."

"It's programmed into my phone."

Lauren's eyes widened. "She gave it to you?"

"Let's say I acquired it." Chris touched her hand. He couldn't help himself. "If you know someone else around here you can call, go ahead."

"I don't know anyone who's here right now. But what about people from your office?"

"Too far away."

"Donna might be by now. We left there over an hour ago."

"It's worth a try, isn't it?"

"I suppose so." Slowly, Lauren opened his contacts on the unlocked phone and scrolled through until she found Donna Delaney's number.

Chris sat close enough to Lauren that he heard the phone ring at the other end of the connection. And ring again. And again.

His body tensed. If she didn't answer or was unable or unwilling to help them, he would have to go to local law enforcement for help. That would tie him up for hours of questioning and waiting and explaining.

"Hello?" Donna Delaney's voice came through loud and clear. "Who is this?"

"It's Lauren."

"What do you want?"

Lauren hesitated a moment. "Help."

"What kind? Putting my son back in prison? No way."

"No, not that." Lauren gave Chris a quick glance before she continued, "Have you heard about the explosion in the parking lot?"

"Of course, I have. It's all over TV." Donna sounded impatient.

Chris hoped that TV was in a friend's house or a hotel room and not the one he had seen in her kitchen.

"That was us." Lauren spoke so softly Chris doubted Donna could hear her.

Silence.

"Are you still there?" Lauren asked.

"I'm here." Mrs. Delaney's sigh sounded like a windstorm through the phone. "Where are you?"

"Ask her where she is," Chris murmured.

"Where are you?" Lauren asked.

"At home making hors d'oeuvres to take to a friend's party tonight."

"Donna, you should—" Lauren stopped. "Please, will you come get us? And bring Saber with you."

"I think you should just call the cops. I don't have time to be running around rescuing you." Donna made her pronouncement and ended the call.

Lauren handed Chris his phone. "Why are we hiding from the police?"

"We're hiding from the press. With an incident like the explosion, they will be wherever law enforcement is."

"And if we end up on camera, whoever is tracking you and me will be able to find us."

"Especially since law enforcement is likely to hold us for longer than is safe now. And I'm not sure we can count on Donna to help us. Or whom else to trust."

Chris didn't feel safe with law enforcement, with others like him, because of her brother. And most of all because he was protecting her.

Her course of action was clear. She needed to get out of the restaurant and away from him to stop being a burden. She had broken their engagement to avoid hindering his chosen career. She still didn't want to interfere with his life.

"I'd like more coffee," she said.

She was telling the truth, but she would have to get it later. While Chris fetched more coffee for them, she would get out of the restaurant. She had left the scene of the explosion with him, too shocked to think what she was doing. Now, with food and caffeine in her system and time and distance since Chris's Jeep had exploded, she was thinking again, her mind and body demanding action.

"I'd like more coffee," she repeated and started to rise.

Chris stood. "I'll get it." He picked up their cups and headed for the drinks counter.

The instant he was around the corner, she stood, snatched her backpack from the other side of the booth and started for the door. If she timed her exit right,

Chris would be preoccupied with filling their cups and wouldn't notice her departure.

Halfway to the door, she remembered the cell phone he had purchased for her. He'd said it was in his coat pocket. She retrieved it, stuffed the phone into her backpack and left the restaurant with a tired-looking family.

A blast of cold air in her face gave her a moment's pause. She was on her own without money or a fully charged cell phone. Bravery or foolishness? She had no idea. She didn't know what she was doing or where she was going except that she needed to separate herself from Chris.

He wouldn't harm her. Never that. But she could never forget how he had been willing to sacrifice their relationship for the sake of a career he had never planned before his father's death. A career he must have known would lie in conflict with his fiancée's family background.

I think I can do more good in law enforcement than as a lawyer, he had said at the time.

He'd accused her of caring about his lower salary expectations. And she had said some hurtful things. She didn't want to remember those. She had replayed them too often over the past five years, regretting every one of them, wanting to apologize, to ask forgiveness.

She could have contacted him. If he had changed his cell phone number, she knew how to find his mother and sister. They would have given him her number for her to apologize.

But she had been carrying around her wounded heart for five years, protecting it by staying away from any kind of contact with Chris. So, was she running now just to be away from him, or because she thought he could go to the authorities without her?

Confused, Lauren slipped between two SUVs and leaned against the bumper of one, out of sight of the restaurant.

Sitting next to Chris at the table had been uncomfortable at best. Too many times, she wanted to rest her head against his broad shoulder, breathe in his scent of soap and fresh air, rest on his strength. When he'd touched her hand, she'd wanted to grasp his fingers and hold tight.

Sitting next to Chris had felt right, which was the source of her discomfort. She shouldn't feel right so close to him.

She felt wrong running away. He would look for her now instead of Ryan. She was wasting his time. He would think that was why she'd left the restaurant without him—to delay him from going after her brother.

Not that he could. Nobody could. Maybe Donna knew, but Lauren had no idea where to find her brother. Just as she had no idea how to get help. She didn't know Donna's phone number to try again with her. All she could do was call the emergency number and ask the sheriff's office to pick her up. Anything else was out of the question. She had no money and no credit cards.

But she did have a credit card. She hadn't yet returned Chris's to him. When she changed her clothes and packed her other purchases in the backpack, she had slipped the card into an outside pocket. She could make her report to the authorities and then somehow get to a hotel for the night. With her and Chris separated, the men who had been able to track them and blow up Chris's car would have difficulty finding them separately.

She hoped.

Slowly, cautiously, Lauren edged toward the parking lot entrance. Walking along the road would make her more visible. But it was safer being out in the open.

She hoped.

She reached the road and picked up her pace. At frequent intervals, she glanced over her shoulder to see if Chris was trying to catch up with her. She looked at the cars speeding past on the road in the event one slowed beside her. If one did, she would run up an aisle between rows of cars in the parking lot next to her.

All this delayed her progress. No matter. She didn't doubt for a moment that officers would remain at the scene of the explosion.

An explosion intended to kill her and Chris.

Lauren shivered. Despite his criminal activities, her father had kept her separate from that part of his life. Violence had never touched her until the night before. It was something she saw happening to other people on the nightly news. Her life was easy because she could afford to make it easy, had worked to have the privilege of security and safety. She wasn't equipped to face down men who wanted her dead. All she knew was to run—from her father, from Chris in his new career, from men who wanted to kill her because of her brother.

This time, she was not running away. She was running toward the law, to someplace quiet where she could work out her feelings toward Chris.

No, not her feelings for Chris. She had no feelings for Chris.

Despite the sunshine once again breaking through the clouds and blazing against white snow and shiny vehicles, making her wish she had purchased sunglasses,

Lauren caught the flash of police lights ahead. Safety. She increased her speed.

And the pocket of her coat vibrated.

She jumped and slipped in a puddle of slush, catching her balance on the side of a compact car. The vibration rippled through the fabric at her hip again. She pulled the cell phone from her pocket and stared at the screen. No name showed, as she hadn't put anything into her contacts, but she could guess the identity of the caller since, as far as she knew, only one person had the number.

For a moment, she debated not answering. The power read only 22 percent. Chris could simply think the phone had died. That, however, wasn't true. The phone hadn't died, and didn't dead phones send calls directly to voice mail? He would think she was avoiding him.

While she argued with herself, the phone stopped ringing, then started again.

She swiped the answer button. "What do you want?"

"That was rude." Chris's voice echoed down the line.

Lauren resumed walking and said nothing. She couldn't dispute what he said. She had been rude in her greeting.

"Why did you leave?" Chris asked.

"I'm going to the sheriff for help."

The sheriff wasn't more than a hundred yards away.

Lauren scowled at an SUV pulling a trailer and blocking her path as it waited on the exit driveway for a break in traffic.

"Did you think of somewhere your brother has gone?" Chris asked.

"I don't know."

"Would you tell me if you did?"

Lauren headed up the driveway so she could walk around behind the trailer and didn't answer. She knew she would. She had to or she would be an accessory to Ryan's crime of escaping federal custody. But Chris wouldn't believe her and the idea of his doubt in her honesty hurt too much. And that hurt made her angry with herself.

She shouldn't care what Christopher Blackwell thought of her.

"Lauren, don't—" The phone beeped to indicate the battery was down to 20 percent and drowned out his next word.

To preserve what power was left, she disconnected the call and dropped the cell phone into her pocket. She had to walk into the parking lot and behind a car and a van to get past the length of the hauler trailer. The car was empty. The van was running, steam puffing from its exhaust pipe and music blaring so loud from inside that the bass pounded into her body like a heavy heartbeat.

She flung up her arm so the driver could see her through the back window and stepped behind the van.

She heard the pop of a disengaged brake at the same time someone shouted, "Stop!"

Too late. She was already behind the van. And the driver had thrown his vehicle into Reverse.

She tried to run. Her boot soles skidded on black ice. No traction. Escape lay too far ahead, too far behind. To her right stood the trailer, to her left the van.

The van surged backward.

Clear pavement lay beyond the trailer's back bumper. She leaped that way. No good. In seconds, she would be a human pancake caught between the van and trailer.

The SUV driver lay on his horn, blasting above the cacophony in the van and the roar of traffic. Other horns resounded from the road.

And suddenly the trailer was gone from her path.

Lauren dived between two cars. A heartbeat later, the van slammed into the vehicles' bumpers, spun onto the driveway and surged into traffic behind the trailer.

Lauren staggered to the front of the cars and was sick in the snowbank.

"It was an accident," she said aloud when she could talk. "An accident."

"Say it enough and we both might believe it." Chris spoke from directly behind her.

That close, he must have been right behind her while calling her. He must have been near enough to see what the van driver intended, must have been the person who warned her.

He must have seen her lose her breakfast in the snow.

Wishing she could simply crawl beneath the nearest sedan, she leaned against the fender instead and covered her face with her hands. "Tell me that was an accident, Chris. Please tell me it was an accident."

She feared she sounded whiny.

"It wasn't an accident, Lauren." Chris brushed hair away from her face with such tenderness tears filled her eyes. "That guy knew you were behind him."

"And he gunned the engine. I heard it." The tears tried to slip out of her eyes and down her cheeks. She squeezed her lids together.

"And who would back up with that trailer right behind him?" His fingertips lingered against her temple, impersonal through gloves, yet oddly intimate, close. "I'm sorry to be so blunt, but I can't lie to you."

"Say what you like. You have always been honest."

"Yes." He heaved a gusty sigh that sounded as though he carried a two-ton weight upon his chest.

She lowered her hands and looked at him. "But the people in the SUV with the trailer. They couldn't have been in on it. And the person in the van couldn't possibly have known I would decide to walk around the trailer and behind him."

"He couldn't have known, no, but he could take advantage of the situation." Chris's eyes, normally bluer than the sun-washed sky, were so somber they were nearly gray.

"Which means he has been looking out for us and I walked right into a trap." Her stomach rebelled again. She swallowed and closed her eyes. "You knew they were around."

"I suspected. It's my job to be suspicious under these sorts of circumstances. But you're smart and quick thinking, which saved you."

"And the fast reactions of the guy in the SUV."

"It was a lady." Chris smiled.

"The person in the van was definitely a man."

Chris's gaze sharpened. "You got a good look at him?"

"I wouldn't say 'good.' The windows were tinted, so I didn't notice hair or eye color, but I'd recognize his profile anywhere. He has a rather prominent nose." She glanced around, fearing she would see the van.

"He's gone for now, but I doubt he's gone far. They're following us."

"How? I didn't notice anyone tailing us to or from Donna's."

"I didn't either, but we used credit cards at the store

and restaurant. They obviously have the ability to track the usage of those."

Lauren's head spun. "Then how can we get away? How can we be safe anywhere?"

"I'm going to go to the nearest ATM and withdraw as much cash as I can, then we will find the nearest sheriff or deputy and tell them the whole story."

Lauren's eyes widened. "You're giving up on looking for my brother?"

"You know I can't do that, Lauren. It's part of my job to apprehend escaped federal prisoners."

"I thought it was also part of your job to protect witnesses. In this case, me."

"I was protecting you until you went out on your own. Lauren—" He looked at the now-cloudless sky, then the cars pulling out of the parking lot, then the slush they stood in, anything other than her. "Lauren, this incident with the van so soon after my Jeep exploded, convinces me they are desperate to see us dead."

"Me?" Lauren pressed her hands to her stomach, willing herself not to be sick again. "But why? I mean, you're the law. I'm just an innocent civilian."

"Are you? Innocent, that is?" Chris looked at her this time, his gaze boring into hers. "Or do you know something about your brother and his activities you're not telling me?"

Lauren's immediate instinct was to lash out at Chris for questioning her honesty yet again. His words hurt. He still didn't trust her. But before she formed the words to defend herself, her thoughts snagged on the idea that maybe Chris was right. Maybe she knew something and wasn't allowing herself to see it.

TEN

One of the most difficult moments in Chris's career thus far had been turning back to the table, seeing Lauren gone and wondering why she felt the need to run away from him. The conclusion had been immediate and devastating.

She either wanted to go to her brother or get information to someone.

She had taken the cell phone. She had kept his credit card. He could have tracked her usage of the card in moments, and by the time he reached anywhere she might have used it, like a car rental service, she could have been long gone, lost on a number of back roads just moments from this heavily populated oasis of commerce near the Great Lakes.

He hadn't expected to find her headed toward the flashing lights of the sheriff's vehicles. Then again, the superstore's parking lot was the best sort of place to hide. It was crowded, and someone might have been willing to give a ride to a woman who could claim her car had been blocked by the explosion investigation. Or, worse, someone could have picked her up there without anyone noticing her, the form of transport or the driver.

Her brother himself could have met her there with no one the wiser. Who would expect a fugitive from the law to enter a zone crawling with law enforcement?

The attempt on her life had left him shaken, his blood boiling. If he had had his weapon, he thought he might have shot out the van's tires so the criminal couldn't have escaped.

But he didn't have his weapon. It had disappeared from Lauren's deck. He thought then that she had it. He wondered now if she did. He wasn't sure how she would have concealed it, but she had worn loose clothes— jeans that were far from skintight, a large flannel shirt over a T-shirt, socks. Yes, he had his arms around her more than once. But only around her waist.

He wondered again now, staring at her bulky sweater and bulkier coat. Easy places to conceal a weapon. And he hated his suspicions, was angry with himself for having them. Yet he was unable to push them aside.

"Lauren, will you be honest with me—"

"I have always been honest with you. You are the one who chooses not to believe me." She pressed the palm of her hand against his chest and pushed past him toward the driveway. "Which is one of the reasons why I knew we could never marry. You have always believed I am more loyal to my brother than to you."

Chris followed her to the back of the cars they had been standing between. "Where are you going?"

"To the police or sheriff deputies or whoever is looking into the explosion of your SUV."

"I'll come with you." Chris fell into step beside her.

"So you can tell them to apprehend me?"

"So I can ask them to help."

"By apprehending me."

"You would be safer in custody."

She shot him a glare. "I hope you're trying to be funny." She hesitated a moment, then said in a voice nearly too soft for him to hear, "You used to be funny."

So he had been. They had laughed a great deal in those two years before his father's murder.

"I don't have much to laugh about these days," he said.

"No lady who makes you laugh? I mean—" She pressed her gloved hand to her lips. "I'm sorry. That's none of my business."

"It's not, but I have no problem answering. I don't."

An young, up-and-coming lawyer had been a catch. A deputy US marshal, not so much.

"When I'm not traveling," he elaborated, "I am trying to find information about my father's death."

"Have you had any kind of a break in that?" The glance she shot him held compassion.

He shook his head. "Details are so scarce and witnesses so hard to find, I suspect someone has tampered with both."

"Someone from inside the Marshals Service?"

"Don't sound so shocked." He didn't mean to sound disdainful, but the tone slipped out before he could stop it. "You know as well as anyone that some people are corruptible regardless of their position. Wasn't one of the charges against your father for bribing a law officer?"

She bit her lip and nodded. "But that one didn't stick."

Which didn't mean it hadn't happened—often. It meant her father was clever enough to cover his tracks well.

"I don't think it's an endemic problem, but it happens." Chris managed to temper his manner this time.

"I'm sorry." She sighed. "For a lot of things."

"Me too." He ached with regrets. "Closure would be nice for my mom and sister and me."

"And catching who did it would bring closure?"

Chris nodded.

"And until that happens everyone is a suspect?"

He flinched as though she'd punched him. "Of course not."

But that sensation of being struck kind of made him feel like a hypocrite for his denial. Ridiculous. Of course he didn't think everyone was guilty of his father's murder, or any other crime. He knew the law. Everyone deserved a fair shake, a presenting of the evidence and questioning of witnesses and all the proper channels of judges and juries before guilt was proclaimed.

Yet he called Ryan Delaney guilty of the crimes of which he had been accused when his only undeniable crime was escaping the courtroom and eluding federal custody.

"Innocent men don't need to flee," he said.

"And neither do innocent women. Enough said."

One of the things he loved—had loved—about Lauren was her outspokenness in their relationship. If he said or did something to hurt her, she called him on it and she expected the same in kind.

There's too much subterfuge in my family for me to continue it in my other relationships, she had explained to him not long after their relationship became serious.

He'd believed her when she said she loved him forever. Then she'd broken off their engagement and said she changed her mind. He didn't know when she spoke the truth after that.

Chris tucked one hand beneath Lauren's elbow to

give her balance as they clambered over a snowbank at the end of the fence surrounding one parking lot. "Where were you headed? I know you said the sheriff, but where did you intend to go after that?"

"A motel."

"Using my credit card."

"I can afford to pay you back."

"But they're tracing our credit cards."

"Of course they are." She sounded weary. "I don't have enough of a criminal mind to have thought of that until you mentioned it. All I could think about was a hot shower and real bed." She rubbed her eyes with the back of her wrist. "Without cash, I guess I can be traced anywhere I go."

"Which is especially dangerous since we don't know why these people want to harm us."

He reached into his pocket to withdraw his credentials. "Let's talk to the sheriff's people now that the media seems to have packed up and gone."

They crossed the access road and stopped where crime scene tape had been strung around the area of the blast. For the first time, Chris saw what was left of his beloved Jeep. Not much identifiable of his SUV or what had been another vehicle beside his, something large that must have protected the next cars along the row. They had broken windows and scarring from flying debris, but were repairable on first glance.

"Were your Christmas presents inside?" Lauren asked.

"They were. And my clothes."

"I'm sorry. I know how it feels to lose your possessions." Lauren rubbed her arms as though she were cold.

She might be. Though the sun was bright enough to melt the top layer of snow—an ice hazard after the sun set—the breeze held an arctic edge. But Chris didn't think that was what made her shiver. He knew the marrow-deep chill spreading throughout his body had nothing to do with the air temperature and everything to do with horror.

They could have been inside when he pressed the starter. They would be dead. Someone else would capture Ryan and no one would continue the pursuit of his father's killer.

The look a young deputy shot them nearly knocked them flat with its hostility. "Move along," he commanded.

Chris held up his credentials. "Deputy US Marshal Christopher Blackwell."

"You got here fast, though we weren't expecting feds." The deputy stalked their way and held out his hand for Chris's wallet. He examined the credentials, then left to talk to a man with white hair and an impressive physique for someone in his fifties at the youngest.

He took the wallet and approached Chris and Lauren. "What are you doing here?"

Not particularly friendly.

"That was my Jeep," Chris said.

And so the questioning began. After ten minutes, Chris suggested they either go to the nearest station or at least into one of the sheriff's SUVs to get out of the cold. They were given the latter option—separate ones. He was glad to see one of the deputies give Lauren a bottle of water. He would have liked one himself, but asking would have lessened him in the eyes of these men who weren't thrilled with his presence anyway.

"I could charge you with leaving the scene," the sheriff said.

"We weren't at the scene." Chris spoke the technical truth, if not the spirit of the truth. "We'd be dead if we had been. Do you happen to have a charger I could borrow for my phone? I need to make some phone calls."

At least he was in the front seat and not the back like a prisoner.

"Depends on what kind of phone you got." The sheriff offered his car charger.

Fortunately, it was compatible and Chris plugged in his phone.

"Now, may I make those calls?"

"To whom?"

"My boss. My mother. And someplace to rent a car."

"You won't find a car rental on Christmas Eve around here, not that'll deliver." The sheriff smirked.

"Then I need someone to take me to one." Chris arched one brow.

"Blessings with that."

Chris suppressed a sigh and looked out the window to where Lauren now sat alone in the other SUV, slumped against the passenger-side window. He hoped she was sleeping. He wished he were sleeping. He had been awake too long to think straight.

"May I make my calls?" he asked.

He hoped the sheriff would leave him alone.

"Go ahead." The man didn't move other than taking his own phone out of his pocket and setting his thumbs flying over the screen.

Resigned to making his calls with an audience, with his half of the conversation being recorded he suspected, Chris called his boss first. "Serious trouble," he began. He concluded with, "What action should I take now?"

"Protect the witness."

"But Delaney—" Chris stopped, knowing the answer.

Others were on it. Others would catch Ryan Delaney.

"And how do you suggest I do that without a vehicle?" Chris asked with an edge he couldn't keep from his voice.

His boss cleared his throat. "We'll get you one. Sit tight." The call ended.

Sit tight within a hundred yards of where someone had tried to crush Lauren between two steel objects. Not an idea that made Chris happy.

Leaving Delaney to others didn't make him happy either.

He glanced at Lauren again. He was unhappy with babysitting duty. Being with her hurt. For five years, he had thought of her and imagined maybe they could eventually be friends or at least break the cycle of anger and resentment toward one another, emotions unhealthy for both of them in mind and spirit. The past day told him neither outcome was likely. Proximity to Lauren had shown Chris the wound she'd dealt him when she broke their engagement wasn't yet healed. It was still raw beneath a far-too-thin layer of scar tissue.

His gaze on Lauren where she was still slumped against the SUV window, Chris called his mother's number.

She answered on the first ring. "Where are you? Are you all right? Do you get to come home soon?"

"I'd rather not say. I'm just fine. And no, I don't think I'll be home before tomorrow at the earliest."

Mom sighed. "We miss you."

"Same here."

He missed her hugs, the way she ruffled his hair like

he was nine, not twenty-nine, the way the house would smell like pine boughs and sugar cookies.

His mouth watered at the thought of his mother's Christmas cookies cut into the shapes of stars and trees and animals. He wanted to tell her how much being around Lauren hurt.

He told her nothing of that personal a nature. Over the phone was not a place for that kind of revelation. In front of the sheriff made the idea of confessing his feelings worse. No one needed to know of his past with Lauren.

So he said goodbye and disconnected the call.

The sheriff opened his door. "Wait here."

He exited the SUV, slamming the door behind him. The deputy met him at the front of the deputy's vehicle and began to talk. Comparing notes on Chris's story with Lauren's.

In the middle of their dialogue, several state vehicles showed up, experts to examine the wreckage of the Jeep to find out what sort of bomb it had been and where it had been planted. Chris wanted to join them, learn what he could, but figured he would merely get in the way. He might as well do as he was told—sit tight, let his phone charge, wait for orders.

And keep an eye on Lauren.

She still appeared to be sleeping. He texted her rather than called in the hope of not waking her up.

Are you all right?

No response.

We'll be out of here soon.

Chris had been assured of transportation and further instructions as to what he should do with Lauren. Probably take her to a motel somewhere remote and guard her. Pay cash so they couldn't be traced. And wait. And wait. And wait.

The idea seemed more like creating a target for whoever wanted to harm her than protecting her. He hadn't done a good job of keeping her safe thus far. Nor had he got anywhere in finding her brother when he had been so close on the lake.

The lake, where Lauren had suggested her brother might go to see his mother.

Chris straightened. She had denied knowing anything about where Ryan would be, and then had come up with his mother's house. Ryan had indeed been there. Would she now come up with another location?

"Your nap is over, my girl." He started to open his door.

His phone rang. Expecting someone from his office, he answered with a curt "Yes?"

"Were you serious when you said some dangerous men might try to get in my house?" The voice spoke in a raspy whisper.

"Mrs. Delaney?" Chris glanced at the caller ID.

"Were you?" How someone could snap in a murmur Chris didn't know, but Donna Delaney managed the feat.

Chris rested his free hand on the door handle, ready to leap out of the SUV at a moment's notice. "Yes, of course I was serious about that. Why—"

"Then they're here." A shaky sigh shuddered over the airways. "They took my dog."

* * *

The slamming door of the other sheriff's vehicle jerked Lauren upright. She must have dozed off in the warmth of the vehicle and being alone, off guard. Her neck stiff, her eyes crusty with sleep, she stared at Chris charging around the hood of the other SUV, a phone clamped to his ear, his voice strong and calm in contrast to the alarm on his face. He headed straight for Lauren's door.

She pushed it open and got out. "What's wrong?"

"We'll wait for you inside the store," Chris said into the phone. "Drive carefully, but come as fast as you can." He ended the call and approached Lauren. "That was Ryan's mother."

Lauren started. "Why did she call you?"

"While she was across the street taking cookies to a neighbor," Chris said, "someone broke into her house and stole Saber."

"Stole that adorable dog?" Lauren staggered back, resting her palms on the side of the SUV for balance. "She's sure? The dog didn't just get out somehow?"

"They left her a message spelled out in Christmas cookies."

"That's just wrong. Sick and wrong on so many levels." Lauren took a long, deep breath to ease the coil of anger in her middle. "Who would use an innocent dog like that? I don't understand such—such depravity. Trying to murder us and burning down my house are one thing. We're human. We can fight back, get help, rebuild. But a dog is innocent and helpless to call for help. Oh." Realizing tears flowed down her cheeks, she wiped them away with the backs of her hands. "Why did they do it? Because Ryan was there earlier today?"

"They want the USB drive."

"The USB drive." Lauren felt like a parrot repeating Chris's words like that, but her brain seemed to be freezing. "Which one?"

"They didn't specify, which makes me think they don't know we have a second one."

"And that little piece of plastic is important enough to them they are willing to kidnap a dog to get it back?"

"They were willing to kill us to get it back."

"But a dog? That sweet, friendly dog in exchange for a bit of plastic and metal?"

"That plastic-and-metal piece must hold some powerful data."

"Like the other one."

Wet from her tears, her hands grew cold. Needing a moment to think, to take in everything that had happened, she retrieved her backpack and gloves from the SUV behind her and donned both. The action didn't help much. Fatigue, a lack of decent food and wondering how someone would try to next kill her raced through her as though each incident were a horse on a carousel spinning, spinning, spinning and going nowhere. She could grab the reins of any one of those whirling horses and have enough to think about and take action on for a week. All of them together left her dizzy and weak, a state she wasn't used to. She had been on her own for the past five years other than occasional visits from her brother. She had built a successful company. She had managed her broken heart without over- or undereating or falling behind in her goal of creating a business that was wholly honest, that protected other businesses against criminal activities like hacking and embezzlement.

But the events of the past twenty-four hours were about to defeat her. Not because she had lost her house, not because she had come so close to death several times, but because these men had picked on a dog with big brown eyes and a wagging tail, the sort of dog Lauren wanted to greet her at the door when she returned from work.

"So how do we get Saber back?" Lauren asked.

"We give them the USB drive."

Lauren stared at him. "It's evidence, isn't it?"

"It is, though its provenance is so compromised it could never be used in a trial. But we don't give them the actual drive—we give them a copy."

"How?" Even as she asked the question, Lauren knew the answer. "So where do we get a computer and the time to make the copy?" She hesitated, then asked the more important question, "And how long do we have to get the USB drive to these guys?"

"Midnight."

Lauren pulled her phone from her pocket and stared at the time. "Twelve hours."

"Can you do it in twelve hours?"

"Maybe. If I have a place to work."

"I'm calling Sheriff Davis to see if he will be helpful again."

"Won't your office mind? And how do we get there?"

"Mrs. Delaney is coming here. As for my office, they've given me the assignment of babysitting, to break off from my pursuit of Ryan Delaney." His tone was too neutral, too flat for that news not to be bothering him.

"Did you tell them you have a past relationship with me? I would think that would convince them you shouldn't have anything to do with me." Her tone was

too edgy to hide her hurt at his dislike of being assigned
to keep her safe.

"It's precisely why they want me watching over you.
They think you are more likely to talk to me than an
officer who is a stranger."

"I have nothing to say that I haven't said already. I
told you about Donna's house."

"Just in time for us not to catch him."

Lauren counted to ten before she dared respond.
"You really do suspect everyone of wrongdoing, don't
you? That has to be a sad way to live your life."

"It's a safe way to live my life."

"You'd rather be safe than have close relationships?"

"My personal life is irrelevant here. Our lives, your
life, depends on me being suspicious." Chris raised his
phone and began to thumb the screen. "I'll call Davis.
Do you mind asking the sheriff if we can go back into
the store? It looks like they didn't shut it down."

"Shut down the only department store for miles on
Christmas Eve? The man wants reelection." Realizing
her comment held too much sarcasm in it to be kind,
she added, "Or maybe he's just compassionate toward
the people here who need to shop for the holiday. And
speaking of shopping…" She pulled his credit card from
her backpack and gave it to him. "I'll pay you back with
interest. I kept the receipts and you can give me the re-
ceipt for the phone."

"Thanks." Chris took the card. "I'm the one who
needs to buy some clothes now." He raised the phone
to his ear.

Lauren slipped past him to find the sheriff or his
deputy.

They were standing guard over the wreckage of the

Jeep and the vehicle next to it. The driving lane to that section had been closed, but cars were allowed to move in and out through the rest of the parking lot. The store was far enough away not to be part of the crime scene. When the bomb had been planted was easy to figure out. Lauren and Chris had been inside the store for at least an hour. Chris had parked in a corner for their safety, and while that had turned out to not be safe at all for the Jeep, it had probably saved dozens of shoppers— men, women, babies. Babies could have been harmed. Lauren held no doubt these men were ruthless enough they would have risked the lives of families to destroy someone they thought had information they didn't want disseminated.

I don't know anything, Lauren wanted to shout at their nameless, faceless enemies.

Ryan hadn't had time to tell her or his mother anything. The first USB drive was full of encrypted information. Lauren suspected the second one would be, as well. So why did these men want her dead and want to control Donna by stealing her dog? She probably knew less than Lauren about the USB drive. Donna hadn't even known of the drive's existence. So what else…

Halfway between the SUV and the sheriff, Lauren halted, her gaze fixed on the distance without seeing anything, her hands clasped behind her, her mind trying to grasp another of those revolving carousel horses. She envisioned a hand reaching for the leather reins draped over a carved and painted wooden mane and a coat of chestnut the same shade as Lauren's hair.

The right question now was, what did she and Donna have in common? The answer was Ryan. Ryan had gone to Lauren, then to his mother. With them out of commission, Ryan had fewer options for finding safe harbor.

Feeling exposed and vulnerable in the middle of the driving lane, Lauren headed for the sheriff at a trot. "Sir, if you don't need to question us further, may we please return to the store? Chris—Mr. Blackwell—needs to buy a few things."

"'Chris,' is it?" The sheriff gave her a narrow-eyed glare. "That seems awfully friendly. Are you two friends?"

"Far from it. Now, may we go into the store?"

"Yes, but don't leave the premises."

"We don't have a car, sir. I don't know how we would leave."

As she returned to Chris, she realized that wasn't true. If Donna was meeting them there, she had to have a car of some sort. Something with four-wheel drive in that climate. Lauren pictured some crossover, feminine car or smaller. Right then, she didn't care if Donna drove a two-seater, as long as it would get them away from the sight of the pile of junk that had been Chris's Jeep and a too vivid reminder of how close they had come to dying.

"What's wrong?" Chris asked when Lauren reached him.

"I was thinking about how close we came to dying." Lauren breathed deeply to calm her jumping stomach. "Twice today alone. And losing my house and all my stuff…"

"Hey, don't freak out on me now." Chris's voice held so much tenderness Lauren wanted to rest her head on his broad chest and cry.

That gentleness came from the Chris she had known and loved, not this harder, cynical federal officer.

She was probably fortunate he was so changed most of the time. If he acted like the old Chris, she would lose all the ground she had gained over five years of reminding herself not to love him. His hardness now protected her heart from further hurt.

Except at that moment when he raised his hand to brush a stray tear from her cheek. Gestures like that punched holes in the protective shell around her feelings for him.

"Let's go." The command barely passed her lips.

"Good idea to get away from here. You don't need to see this."

"The sheriff told us not to leave the area."

"He has no reason to hold us here. We've given our statements." Chris stepped aside so she could precede him between cars. "Sheriff Davis says we are welcome to return there and use their computer. He said it's a quiet as a—that it's quiet there."

As quiet as a what? Grave? Tomb?

She understood why he stopped himself from saying one of those things. They had been too close to death to use the term lightly.

"Donna will be here in an hour or so?" Lauren asked.

"And so will someone from the nearest marshal's office to deliver a vehicle of some sort to me."

"So what do we do with Donna?" Lauren glanced around the parking lot, noting how little the crowds had thinned.

Seemed like everyone had waited until the last minute to Christmas shop or buy groceries for parties or family dinners.

Lauren hadn't enjoyed a family dinner since she was a teen. And *enjoyed* wasn't the right word for it. They had been catered affairs with cousins she never saw the rest of the year, many of whom looked at her like some sort of pariah. She was the daughter of the "other woman," and most of her cousins had preferred Donna. The majority would end up senseless from drinking too much, and she spent the time in her room as soon as she could escape.

Except for the Christmas she'd spent with Chris's family.

She slammed the door on that memory and followed Chris into the store. This time she was the one to go to the cell phone kiosk to buy him a car charger and charge her own battery while she waited. Once done with that, she located the electronics section to buy a USB drive with cash Chris had given her.

Since one exactly the same wasn't available, she found one as close to the original as she could locate and hoped the men who had kidnapped an innocent animal wouldn't know the difference. If they had never seen the original USB drive, they were all right. If they had and understood the differences...

She would figure out something. She would not allow that poor puppy to be harmed.

An imbedded self-destruct sequence on the drive would be her insurance to convince them to turn over the dog. She wasn't sure she could pull something like that off in this short amount of time, but she would certainly try.

Which led her to wonder why they wanted the USB drive so badly. Surely they knew the data had been extracted from the other one and she and Chris would have enough time to obtain data from this second one. That meant the data the devices held still mattered regardless of who else knew about it.

She wished she knew what that data was. No doubt the cryptologists for the government would never release the information so she could find out. But she was safer not knowing anyway.

Safer. That was a joke these days.

The same sense of vulnerability she'd experienced in the parking lot washed over her again. The man buying video games might not be a father picking up some last-minute gifts for his children as he claimed. He might be following her, seeking an opportunity to harm her. The two women in designer coats and boots purchasing a wide-screen television might in truth be accomplices with the men who had pursued her and Chris. Lauren wasn't even certain those were men. The driver of the van had a chiseled profile she had seen, but it could belong to a woman with strong facial bones as much as to a man.

She. Could. Not. Live. Like. This.

Glancing over her shoulder several times, she scurried to the front of the store to meet Chris. He stood in line already, and she hastened to join him despite several mean looks from those behind.

"I found—" She started to tell him she'd found a USB drive close to the appearance of the original one, then stopped herself.

Two men, a generation apart, stood in the line ahead of her and Chris. A mother and two small children followed behind. The mom was probably all right, but the men were dubious.

She might not want to live her life like this. For the

moment, however, she had no choice if she wanted to stay alive.

She said nothing until they'd paid for their purchases and left the store. "Why are the USB drives so important?"

"I've been wondering that myself." Chris scanned the parking lot. "What does Mrs. Delaney drive?"

"I have no idea. Something feminine, I bet."

"Like a pink Cadillac?"

Lauren smiled. "Not that feminine. But about the data. It's important enough they want it even though they know we've had time to get it."

"Names? Locations? If they have the key for breaking the encryption, they could get to locations or people before us."

"Of course. Then we should make sure they don't have access to the data." She began to rethink her plans.

"Let's sit on that bench." Chris pointed to a bench against the outside wall of the store and tucked behind a support post for the overhang. "I feel a little too exposed just standing here."

They started for the bench, but Chris's phone rang. He answered it. "We're at the front of the store. Is the baby blue compact—" His eyebrows shot up. "Okay, I see you."

Lauren followed his gaze and her own eyes widened.

Donna drove a Yukon.

"Park it," Chris said into the phone.

The black Yukon roared past, Donna giving the horn a brief tap.

And behind her by two cars rumbled a black truck with oversize tires.

ELEVEN

"**G**et inside, Lauren." Chris didn't need to tell her what to do. She was already moving, speed walking so she didn't run over anyone, not waiting for the automatic doors to open all the way before she slipped through. Her orange backpack disappeared behind the glass, and Chris focused his attention on Donna Delaney and the truck in pursuit.

He hadn't seen the vehicle in daylight. He hadn't got a license plate. He had no reason to think this was the same truck that had blocked Lauren's driveway the night before, then sat on the road waiting for him and Lauren. Yet he knew it was with the gut instinct that had saved his bacon more than once.

Now it idled between him and Mrs. Delaney's Yukon, its windows too tinted for Chris to see more than the driver's profile—and the silhouette of a large dog sitting up in the back seat—from where he stood half-behind a support pillar. The post wasn't much protection if the man started shooting. Only one person seemed to be inside the truck though. Chris could manage one man. Better if he had his weapon.

Slowly, Chris edged toward the truck. It had pulled

up to the curb as though intending to pick up a passenger. He would feel like a fool if this were some innocent man waiting for his wife. But he would be more foolish if he didn't try to apprehend this man, service weapon on hand or not.

He reached out one hand to knock on the window—

And the truck peeled back into the lane of traffic, narrowly missing the fender of a Camry. The Camry driver blasted his horn. Nothing to the truck driver. He kept going.

And Chris got a camera shot of his license plate.

It was muddy and salt-encrusted, but readable because the vehicle sat up so high it had missed most of the road grime. He could text the picture to his office and trace the truck. Finally, a break. The driver of the truck had made a mistake exposing himself to—

A scream reverberated from inside the store, drowning the strains of "Blue Christmas" and the cacophony of blasting horns and excited children.

For a beat, Chris didn't move. Couldn't move. Then he whirled on his heel and raced for the store, elbowing his way past shoppers, ignoring their protests.

"Mr. Blackwell, what's going on?" Donna Delaney's smoke-roughened voice rang out behind him.

He motioned for her to come inside with him and kept moving, charging for the source of the scream, for the crowd surrounding a woman kneeling on the floor, clutching an orange backpack to her chest.

"Lauren." He tapped a store security guard on the shoulder. "She's with me. What happened?"

"Not sure. I heard her scream, but by the time I got here, she was like this."

"Lauren?" Chris crouched in front of her. "What happened?"

"Have to have attention, just like your mother." Donna towered over Lauren.

The accusation galvanized Lauren more than Chris's gentle question. Her head shot up. She stared wide-eyed at the crowd around her as though she hadn't realized anyone was there, then tried to stand.

"Let me help." Chris offered his hand.

"I can hold your bag for you, miss." The security guard reached for the backpack.

Lauren clutched it more tightly. "It's mine." She grasped Chris's hand and he drew her to her feet. "Thanks."

He kept hold of her fingers. "You're shaking."

"What happened, miss?" the security guard asked.

"I'm not sure." Lauren met Chris's gaze with a question or a plea.

He guessed a plea. She didn't want to tell the security guard something. She didn't want to talk about it with a stranger because it had something to do with the pursuit, with them as the quarry.

"She probably slipped on the floor," Donna said.

"It's not wet." The security guard rubbed his own foot across the concrete.

"It's all right. Please forgive me." Lauren gave the guard such a warm smile the tips of his ears reddened.

"If you're sure, miss. I can fill out an incident report."

"We don't have time for incident reports." Donna grasped Lauren's arm. "We need to go."

Chris wasn't sure whether Donna acted impatient to help or because she truly thought they should be on their way. A jumping muscle beneath her eye suggested she wanted to be away.

Frowning and glancing about as though afraid someone would swoop in and tell him he was making the wrong move, the security guard took a step back. "All right, then. Be careful."

"I intend to be," Lauren murmured. "Where are we going? Donna's car?"

"I'd rather not. If that truck belonged to the men after us, they followed Mrs. Delaney here." Chris glanced at his phone for messages. "Someone is supposed to deliver a vehicle for us."

"So, how do we get my dog back?" Donna demanded. "I don't know anything about a USB drive. I don't even know what a USB drive is."

"This." Lauren drew one from the plastic bag hanging from her wrist.

Donna shrugged. "Never used one."

"But Ryan left one in your house this morning."

"He couldn't have. He wasn't in my house this morning."

"He took his skates," Chris pointed out.

"He wasn't there," Donna insisted. "I was home all morning and I didn't see him."

"Then how did he take the skates so fast?" Chris asked.

"I don't know." Donna met his gaze so directly he thought she just might be telling the truth. "Why would he cut across the lake in the first place?"

"Harder to catch than if he kept to the road," Chris said. "And doesn't he have a key?"

"Of course, but—" Donna's shoulders slumped. "I guess he sneaked in while I was at the back door putting Saber out. My own son acting like a thief." She blinked hard. "Can we get out of here?"

"We should move along before that guard comes back to ask what we're doing loitering." Chris scanned the store.

The least likely place for anyone to be on Christmas Eve was…? Where? Hardware? Automotive?

"Let's go." He gestured for the ladies to precede him.

They traversed several aisles until they reached the back wall. A line of tools hung on the wall, large gaps showing where the supply had been diminished for Christmas gifts. For a flash, Chris yearned for his father's presence. Tools had always made him happy as gifts. The man loved to build things, from bird feeders to bookshelves.

He shoved the sadness and memories aside in an instant. This was not the time to be sentimental or personal.

"What happened, Lauren?" He posed the question a little more abruptly than he intended, but he needed to focus his mind on something besides those empty tool shelves.

"Someone grabbed my backpack." Lauren slipped her arms through the straps, then hugged her middle as though cradling those straps against her. "They yanked me backward when they did it, so I threw my head back and bashed either their nose or chin and screamed. He shoved me to the floor and took off."

"He?" Chris asked. "Did you see him?"

"Just his feet and legs."

"He could have been a common thief," Chris mused aloud. "With a hard yank, you can pull a backpack off someone."

"I knotted the straps so that's not as easy." Lauren moved her arms and he saw the ends of the straps were looped so they couldn't slide through the buckles.

"So you got attacked by some thief, while some hoodlums took my dog over a piece of plastic."

"I think they were after more than a piece of plastic." Chris studied Lauren's face, wondering how much more she could bear. "I think that truck was a distraction so you could be attacked, maybe even forced to go with one of them."

"Then why just grab my backpack?" Lauren asked.

"I don't know." Chris shoved his fingers into his hair, wincing at how the tape from the bandage pulled. "But I can tell you I don't think we should get separated like that again." He glanced at Donna. "That includes you until we get your dog back."

And Ryan captured. If this ended with Ryan captured.

The idea that Ryan's capture might not end this nightmare left Chris feeling sucker punched.

"So how do we get my dog back?" Donna asked a second time.

"We have a plan. I'd rather not say what it is here. Once someone brings me a vehicle—"

On cue, the text alert sounded from his phone. He glanced at the screen. His replacement vehicle was in the parking lot. On the far side from the crime scene. A picture accompanied the text. It showed a battered Jeep. No remote starter for something that old. They would be blessed if the heater still worked. Another text told him where to find the key with the admonition, Don't lose it. There isn't another one.

So he wouldn't meet whoever had dropped it off.

No one would see one man get out of the vehicle and a man and two women get in. By the time Chris and his party reached the SUV, the marshal who had dropped it off would be somewhere guarding it from out of sight and the constant flow of shoppers would have changed. General enough precautions, but they didn't account for the possibility—the likelihood—that he and the ladies were being watched, that someone might follow them the instant they left the store.

"Let's look for an exit that isn't the loading dock or the front door." He started to pace the perimeter.

"What's wrong with the front door?" Donna's boot heels clicked on the polished surface of the floor.

Chris glanced down. She wore boots better suited to a party than walking through snow and ice. No doubt she had dressed up to deliver cookies to neighbors.

His mother would be doing the same thing. His mother and sister would be alone for the holiday.

This wasn't the first time he left them on their own because of work. It wasn't the only holiday they had celebrated without him: Thanksgivings, Independence Days...

How many holidays had Lauren celebrated alone?

He glanced at her. She trudged beside him, her head bent so her hair covered her face.

"What good will another exit serve?" Donna asked again from behind them.

"They can't cover all of them at once, I don't think. There will be at least one more exit, maybe two." Chris thought for a moment. "The least likely to be guarded is one that is for fire exit only."

"That'll set off an alarm," Lauren said.

"Probably, but we'll be behind cars in the lot before

anyone gets there to investigate." Chris stopped to let a gaggle of teen girls, laughing and teasing one another, scoot past with their arms full of Christmas ornaments. "Haven't you ever noticed how long those alarms usually ring before anyone shuts them off?"

The ladies didn't respond as they passed bedding, then housewares. Then they reached clothing and dressing rooms. Beyond those, a door with an emergency-exit sign above it hid in a corner.

"Walk out and go around the corner, then cross to the cars and get between them as fast as you can without running." Chris knew Lauren would follow his instructions. Donna was another matter. "Don't argue with me, Mrs. Delaney. We are trying to stay safe and get your dog back."

"If they haven't killed her already."

"They haven't. She was in the truck."

Donna's face lit. She might not be all that nice to Lauren, the daughter of the woman who had stolen her husband, but she loved her dog.

"Okay, let's go."

The area was deserted, making their exit easy. Fortunately. The instant Lauren pressed the panic bar on the door, an alarm began to blare. If any of the men after them were in the store, they might suspect what had happened. Chris could only hope and pray he found the SUV provided for him before anyone caught up with their location.

Ahead of him, the ladies were gone. He waited, ensuring they got away safely, then slipped out behind them and speed walked as Lauren had before, covering a great deal of ground in a short period of time without drawing the attention running did. He caught up with

Lauren and Donna in moments. From behind the pickup truck they had chosen for cover, he counted rows, spotted the Jeep, compared it to the picture on his phone.

"Right there." He pointed it out to the ladies.

"Does it run?" Lauren asked.

"I expect it runs perfectly, but I can't guarantee any other luxuries." Chris shepherded them before him. He would have felt better with his gun, something he still needed to talk to Lauren about.

She couldn't possibly have it. He couldn't be thinking straight to believe for a moment she would have taken it. She hated guns, had said so often in the past.

And yet...

Regardless, he needed to get them all away as quickly as possible.

He found the key in a magnetized case inside the right rear wheel well and clicked open the door locks. "Go ahead and get in." He popped the back and dropped in his purchases, then rummaged through the bag to find the car charger for his cell.

"I'll sit in the back," Lauren was saying. "I don't mind at all."

"You won't be able to talk to your deputy US marshal." Donna's tone held a sarcastic note that made it more taunting than teasing.

Lauren maintained silence on that subject. Chris could guess what she was thinking, though—*I have nothing to say to him.*

Once upon a time, they had barely been able to stop talking to one another. As he slammed the back hatch and rounded the Jeep to climb into the driver's seat, he admitted he missed those days. She hadn't simply been his girlfriend. She had been his best friend.

Yet he had made a major life decision without talking it over with her first. He had kept his application to the US Marshals Service secret. When he received his job offer, he had accepted the position, then resigned from his law firm before he told Lauren of his decision.

That had been arrogant and stupid. He should tell her that. Maybe if he had discussed it with her, she would have understood and supported his decision.

And pigs were going to start flying any minute now. In no way would she have supported his decision. Deputy US marshals who wanted promotion didn't marry the daughters of felons. He had known that. So why had he believed he and Lauren would be different?

Wishful thinking. They had shared so much—the same faith, the same love of lakes and snow and strategy games before a roaring fire and so much more. He had hoped they could overcome anything.

But he had shut her out of his decision.

Maybe if he admitted he'd been wrong, she would at least like him again.

Feeling like a teen with his first crush, Chris slid into the driver's seat and slipped the key into the ignition. He started to turn it to start the car.

"Don't." From the back seat, Lauren grabbed his arm.

Lauren knew she was being silly. She knew she should let go of Chris's arm and let them get away from the parking lot, away from the last sighting of the men trying to kill them—or at least her. But she couldn't make her fingers open enough to release him. Her hand clutched his well-formed biceps, shaking at the idea of what could happen to them if Chris turned that key.

"Lauren." He shifted in his seat and covered her hand

with his free one. "We're all right. The Jeep's all right. It was thoroughly inspected less than a half hour ago and has been under total surveillance since."

"I know. I know, but—"

"Knock it off," Donna commanded. "Grow a spine."

Lauren had never considered she was missing backbone, lacking courage, until that moment when she couldn't bear the idea of Chris turning the ignition only to have the SUV explode in a hail of flaming steel and fuel. She looked into Chris's lake-blue eyes and realized what a coward she had been in their relationship. She'd claimed she loved him, but her fears had kept her from supporting him in the career he'd felt led to pursue.

"I'm sorry." She managed to release his arm, but her apology ran so much deeper than for preventing him from starting the Jeep.

"It's all right. Put your seat belt on." Chris faced forward and turned the key.

The SUV roared to life without blasting them all to fragments.

Lauren released her breath in a gusty sigh.

"You're just like your mother," Donna said. "She couldn't face the truth either."

Lauren clutched her knees. She couldn't argue with Donna.

Momma had run the instant her husband was arrested. She had claimed she didn't think him guilty of money laundering and attempted murder, then packed up everything of value she could lay her hands on and vanished.

Her daughter didn't hold enough value to take with the silver candlesticks and Waterford crystal.

"What truth is Lauren running away from?" Chris asked.

"She knows. She'll tell you if she has the courage. Now, where are we going?"

"To someplace safe." Chris's answer was as evasive as Donna's.

Lauren wanted a straight answer from Donna. She wasn't sure herself from what truth she was allegedly running.

"Seems to me," Lauren said, "that you were the one running away from the truth when you denied Ryan was in your house."

"I can't believe he wouldn't have spoken to me," Donna said.

"He was protecting you." Lauren picked at a frayed edge of vinyl on the armrest. "He is good at protecting those he cares about."

"Then why did he lead those men straight to both of you?" Chris sounded angry.

"Because something else was more important to protect." Lauren spoke slowly as the ideas slogged through her exhausted brain. "He needed to get information to us that is bigger than we are."

"What's more important than his mother?" Donna nearly whined that one. "May I smoke if I open the window?"

"No." Chris's answer was resounding. "This is federal property."

Donna sighed with frustration.

Lauren sighed with relief.

"Keeping lots of people safe at once is bigger even than his mother," Lauren suggested. "A whole neighborhood of people or a city."

"Or a country," Chris said.

"Ryan wouldn't know anything about criminals trying to harm any large number of people." Donna removed a cigarette from her purse and stuck it between her lips. "He sold real estate, not state secrets."

"It doesn't have to be state secrets to affect many people," Chris said.

Donna and Chris bantered back and forth about what those possibilities could be. Lauren tuned them out, planning the steps she needed to take once she had the USB drive and a computer. Every moment proved a struggle not to fall asleep. Other than a couple of cat-naps, she hadn't slept since the previous morning. She didn't think Chris had slept at all either. Nor Ryan, wherever he had gone. Whyever he had gone. Ryan, the one person not to abandon her, had taken himself out of her reach with his actions.

Except Chris hadn't truly abandoned her. She had sent him away. For five years she had bolstered her broken heart with the tale of how Chris had made their future impossible with his actions. Though he was wrong to have made a new and major career move without so much as telling her, she was the one who'd slammed the door on their future.

The right move for him. She had done it for him. He would have an easier time not being married to Richard Delaney's daughter. She'd gained nothing by ending their engagement—nothing but heartache and loneliness.

If her heart could still ache, she must still care.

Not liking the direction of her contemplations, Lauren focused her mind on solving the USB drive problem. That carried her all the way to her own territory, the town near where her house had stood for more than fifty years and the friendly sheriff's department.

"What am I supposed to do while you're messing about on the computer?" Donna asked.

"Read magazines?" Lauren eyed the suggested items and caught herself half smiling over the idea of her half brother's mother reading sporting periodicals.

Donna's look should have frozen Lauren to the lobby floor. From the corner of her eye, she caught Chris's half smile and was warmed enough to counter Donna's coldness.

Dangerous. Very dangerous to have so slight a gesture affect her that way.

She couldn't care for him. Not again. Nothing had changed. In fact, things were worse with Ryan's arrest and now-fugitive status. She'd always be Richard Delaney's daughter, despite her name change.

She turned from Chris and Donna to Sheriff Davis, who appeared somewhat more rested. "Where would you like me to work?"

"Same place. I'm sorry it's not more private, but we're a little constrained on space."

"Not a problem. I don't need privacy."

She had started her career working in cubicles with only a pretense of privacy coming from six-foot walls on three sides. Early on, she learned to tune out her surroundings and concentrate on only the screen in front of her.

Her eyes felt so scratchy from lack of sleep she wondered if she could do that much. She must. More than saving a dog's life depended on her convincing these men they were receiving the USB drive. This was the US Marshals' chance to catch the men who were determined to hurt one of their own either for himself or because he was with Lauren.

That data must be terribly important for the men to risk being caught. Surely they knew that and suspected many would think a dog was expendable.

Not to Lauren. Nor, apparently, to Chris.

She wished she felt safe where she was. She told herself she should, that she was just fine. Those men didn't know the vehicle Chris, Donna and she had left the store in. They wouldn't consider the three of them would return to the sheriff's office. The space was well protected—more or less.

She eyed the wide window in front of her and hoped it was bulletproof glass. Now in daylight, she saw more clearly how vulnerable it was from the street. The door, though it was steel, appeared suddenly too defenseless, the deputy stationed by it too young and flimsy to be of any use against someone trying to break in.

"Lauren?" Chris was beside her, one hand resting on her shoulder. "Are you all right?"

She realized she was gripping the desk with both hands, her knuckles white.

"Breathe," Chris said. Lauren inhaled to the bottom of her lungs, letting it out slowly.

"Again. Slowly so you don't hyperventilate." Chris's voice was soothing, calming.

She breathed deeply and slowly yet again. Some of the tension in her chest released.

"Will you look at me?"

She raised her gaze to his and a different sort of tightness filled her middle. She could drown in those lake-blue eyes and be happy. She was drowning now, sinking, falling, falling—

She snapped her focus away. "I'm okay now. It's just that window... Anyone walking past..." She gestured to the expanse of glass.

"I'll ask Davis if we can lower the shade."

"Not much protection against bullets," Lauren said.

"I presume the glass is bulletproof." Chris removed his hand from her shoulder. "Can you work here?"

"I don't have much choice, do I?" Lauren managed a smile for him without meeting his eyes again.

She wanted to tell him to go away, move out of her sphere. She might be able to tune out the defenselessness she felt with that window twenty feet away, but she was still too susceptible to his nearness.

Five years of carefully not thinking about him down the drain in less than a day. Proximity, needing one another to stay safe and alive, helping him—

Helping him catch her brother and put him in prison again.

She had to do it. Sadly, this was the right action. Ryan's behavior was unacceptable. Maybe it wasn't as unacceptable as their father's, but it was wrong in the eyes of the law and society. She had to face that. Innocent men didn't need to run from justice.

Unless they have a really good reason.

That quiet voice niggled at a corner of her mind. What if he had a good reason for running?

She couldn't think of one.

She didn't have time to think of one. She needed to get to work. *Focus. Focus. Focus.*

She set up the computer to protect its contents, then took the USB drive from Chris and began to work. As always when she got before a monitor, her ability to concentrate took over. Sound faded. Sight of everything else disappeared.

Somewhere along the way, someone wrapped her hand around a mug of hot soup. She sipped and typed, sipped and typed. The heat soothed her jumpy stomach. And the mug never seemed to empty, though the contents changed. Hot chocolate, rich and sweet. More soup. Coffee. She drank. She typed. She hacked through passwords too complex to be amateur. She didn't think about who was taking care of her.

The bang sent her shooting the wheeled chair backward. Her mug crashed to the floor. She would have followed had Chris not appeared beside her and grasped her hand.

"It's all right. Just a fender bender in the street."

"You're sure?" She blinked at him, avoiding his eyes.

"I'm sure." He released her hand as though it scorched him. "There's ice out there now that the sun's gone down."

"The sun's gone down?" She stared at the line of darkness around the edge of the shaded window. "How long have I been working?"

"About three hours."

"Awful way to spend Christmas Eve," Donna said from inside the break room.

She sat on the sagging sofa with her feet propped on a chair, knitting needles in hand.

She had brought knitting with her? She had fled her house with needles and yarn?

Lauren had fled her house with nothing, and that was exactly what she possessed from her lake house, her true home.

Her gaze fell on the orange backpack shoved beneath

the desk. She had a change of clothes, a hairbrush and a toothbrush. She had an impersonal condo in Grand Rapids where she could be near an airport for work. The lake house had been home.

She rubbed her eyes. "It is a terrible way to spend Christmas Eve. I'm sure your mother and sister are missing you, Chris."

"I've talked to them. They're going to church and a party afterward."

"But I'm sure they would rather have you there."

She would have liked to be there, in a house smelling of a pine tree and gingerbread cookies.

She rose. "Let me take a break and then I'll get back to work so you can get back to your family."

She went into the ladies' room to wash her face and pull her hair back into a ponytail. What she'd give for a shower and shampoo. For a bed and about twenty hours of sleep.

For an end to being the quarry in someone's game of pursuit.

She returned to the computer to find a fresh cup beside the keyboard. More hot chocolate. She went back to work. Type. Sip. Type.

And suddenly she was staring at a screen that was not the gibberish of an encrypted file.

TWELVE

"Chris."

Lauren's soft cry throbbed with an emotion he couldn't interpret. Panic? Excitement? Either way, his name on her lips drew him to her side in a flash.

"What is it? Did you—" The words on the screen stopped him from speaking as fast as a hand across his lips.

Not words, but names. First names, last names, street names. The words came after the names and addresses, a description of what action was intended against each man—*elimination*.

"I'm presuming *elimination* is the same as *assassination*," Lauren said in a whisper.

"Yes." Chris studied each name. "I don't recognize a single name though. Do you?"

The look she shot him held disappointment and pain. "Of course I do. I had them all over for tea last week so we could discuss how we would take over the world." Her tone held the bite of sarcasm.

"I didn't think they were your friends. I just thought…" Chris pressed the heels of his palms to his aching temples.

He couldn't say what he thought—that she might recognize the names because these men listed might be friends of her father or her brother. She wouldn't take well to the accusation. She shouldn't. It was unfair to her. He had been unfair to her. He wanted to heal the rift between them, and all he managed to do was make matters worse.

"Of course you wouldn't know these men." He dropped his hands to his pockets.

"They aren't on some wanted list?" Lauren asked.

"That's the FBI's list, not ours. Are there more, or just these on this screen?"

She scrolled the display. Two dozen more names Chris didn't recognize went past. By Lauren's lack of reaction, he guessed she knew none of them...until they reached the bottom. Then she flinched hard enough Chris saw her body jerk.

They both knew the three names at the bottom of the monitor.

Richard Delaney

Ryan Delaney

Lauren Wexler

"My dad. My brother. Someone wants to kill us."

Chris clasped his hands behind his back to stop himself from drawing her into his arms.

"I'm only on this list because I'm related to these men." She sounded young, vulnerable, not unlike the day she told him who her father was and that he had been to prison.

My dad is a crook. He says he's a legitimate businessman now, but I think he's just got smarter about how he launders money.

She hadn't looked at him then. She didn't look at him now. She reached to touch the screen of the monitor above her name, then snatched her hand back as though the glass scorched her.

Chris wanted nothing more than to wrap his arms around her and hold her, protect her with his life, not because he had been ordered to do so, but because he could think of nothing he wanted more than to protect her from the present danger, from her past, from the mistake he had made in letting her go.

He had to be satisfied with drawing a chair up beside her and taking her hands in his. "They won't harm you. I promise that with my life."

"I wish you were only speaking figuratively instead of literally." Her hazel eyes were huge and dark, the pupils dilated. She clutched his fingers hard enough to hurt, a feat considering her hands were half the size of his. "Chris, why?"

"I don't know. I can only guess they think you know something they need kept quiet."

"I don't know anything. I haven't seen Ryan since months before he was arrested, though I did talk to him briefly when he was out on bail. And as for my father, I haven't seen him in years."

"But you're a computer-security expert. Maybe they think you have helped them from a distance and locked down the information so it can't be hacked."

"Whoever they are." She glanced toward the front window. "I feel vulnerable here. Is there someplace we can go that's more secure?"

"Is there somewhere we can go that's more comfortable?" Donna's heels clacked toward them. "And what about my dog—what's all that?" She nodded toward the monitor.

Lauren touched a button on the keyboard and the data on the screen vanished. "Nothing to do with you."

Chris hoped she was right. He hadn't seen Donna's name on the list, but they hadn't scrolled to the next screen. They had stopped on Lauren's name.

She glanced from him to Donna to the monitor, and he suspected she had the same thought. If Ryan had information these men wanted, they might fear Donna had known it too. That meant the exchange with the dog and USB drive was likely a trap for them, not the other way around as Chris had hoped.

"Let me see what I can do." He rose and crossed the lobby to knock on Davis's door. When told to enter, he slipped inside to find the sheriff seated behind his desk, reading a file. "How much crime do you have around here?"

"Not much. A few break-ins of summer homes, speeders, some shoplifting." Davis set the folder aside. "What can I do for you?"

"Do you know of a motel that might have rooms?"

"Not near here. Your ladies need a nap?"

"We need someplace secure."

Davis rubbed his chin, whiskers rasping. "There's my place."

"But your family…"

Chris wasn't dragging anyone else into this debacle.

"No family there." Davis stood. "I have a lot of family around here, but I live alone in the woods. I have a fence to keep the deer out of my garden, and there's a back road out. You all can shower and sleep." He glanced toward the front desk, where Lauren sat with her face buried in her folded arms, sleeping or crying. Chris hoped it was the former and feared the latter. Donna perched on the corner of the desk, swinging one long, booted leg as though she were sixteen, not sixty. "What about fetching the dog?"

"I'll take care of that."

"Alone?"

Chris shrugged.

"You're sure it's not a trap? I mean, I love dogs. Had one of my own until a month ago, and plan to get another soon. But it's a risk."

"It's a trap. I can only hope to spring it on them instead."

"I'll come with you."

"It's not your jurisdiction."

Davis waved his hand, dismissing that notion. "I'll have two of my men watch the ladies and go with you."

"On Christmas Eve?"

Davis shrugged. "I'll take you all out to my house, make an appearance at the family Christmas party, then join you. That work?"

"It works for me."

Chris wasn't sure it worked for his office, but what they didn't know wouldn't harm anyone.

That thought gave him pause. If he was acting without permission, something was wrong with his job. This work had been his life for five years. He had made no moves without being given orders, except for trying to dig into files to discover more about his father's murder. That was a far cry from taking action without informing his supervisor.

They had said to keep the ladies safe, and that was what he was doing. The dog was something different. The service wasn't going to waste resources on rescuing a dog.

But Davis intended to, and Chris would because he wanted the opportunity to catch these men and stop them—before they harmed the lady he had once loved enough to want to spend the rest of his life with, a lady he had discovered this past day he still cared about.

Maybe too much for his own good.

Davis glanced at the clock. "The next crew will be coming in half an hour."

"I'll tell the ladies." Chris turned from the doorway, took a step toward Lauren and froze.

He really needed sleep if he was hearing things. No way had he just heard a dog bark. Yet it sounded again. Quick. Urgent.

And then Donna slammed to her feet and ran toward the rear door of the office—the parking lot side—her heels clattering like hoofbeats on a sound stage, her cry of "Saber" ringing through the rooms.

"Wait." Chris sprinted after her and blocked her path to the door. "Wait."

"But it's my dog. I know her bark." Donna's face glowed with joy.

"I believe you. I also think it could be a way to lure us into the open."

A way to ensure they were at the sheriff's office, a message to say, "We know where you are. You can't hide."

"Let Davis get her." Chris stepped aside to allow Davis and a deputy, service weapons in hand, to move past him and Donna and reach for the door.

"Camera only shows the dog," Davis said. "But someone could be hiding in the trees."

Or planting another bomb in Chris's Jeep. Or, worse, planning an assault from the front.

"Lauren." Chris called her name and raced down the corridor to find her with her head still down on the desk. He touched her shoulder, and she startled. Her head shot up to show eyes blurred with sleep.

"Get up. Quick." Chris tucked his hands beneath her elbows and lifted her from the seat.

"What? What's wrong? What happened?" Her voice was rough from her nap and she stumbled against him.

He wrapped his arms around her and spun her away from exposure to the windows, then released her except for her hand and pulled her into the windowless break room. "Sorry for the manhandling. It seems Saber has been dropped off, and I was afraid they might be distracting us in the back to attack from the front."

"They tried that trick in the store and it didn't work." She rubbed her eyes. "But it means they know where we are."

"It does."

"How can we get anywhere else? They'll follow us."

"I have an idea about that. If Davis is willing—"

The *click* of dog toenails on tile racing toward them interrupted Chris. Seconds later, a sixty-plus-pound black Labrador flung herself into Chris's arms. He laughed for the first time in days, then dropped to his knees to pet the dog into calmness.

Donna appeared around the corner, and Saber raced to fling herself against her person's legs.

"Saber, sit," Donna commanded in a quiet, firm voice.

Saber obeyed, gazing at Donna with devotion, her mouth agape in a canine grin.

"She's adorable," Lauren murmured.

With the softness of her face, Chris thought Lauren was adorable, beautiful.

Lovable.

And he knew in that moment he was in trouble. Five years away from her had made no difference in how he felt about Lauren Wexler. He still loved her. He had not for one moment stopped loving her. He wouldn't stop loving her in a lifetime.

And none of the circumstances that had driven them apart had changed. If anything, they were worse.

Heart heavy, Chris left the ladies to play with the dog and talked to Davis about what they had found in the parking lot and how they could get safely anywhere.

"Someone was out there," Davis informed Chris. "We heard him running around the corner, but he was gone across the street before we could catch him."

"And now they're out there watching for us to be careless. Are you willing to take some fairly aggressive measures to get us out of here safely?"

"Frankly, I'd rather have you out of here." Davis grinned to take the sting out of his words.

Chris told him his plan. And when the next shift arrived, they put it into action.

Department SUVs went out to stop traffic in both directions. Another deputy took off in Chris's Jeep. Then Chris, Lauren and Donna, along with Saber, piled into the back of a department vehicle, keeping below the windows, and headed in the opposite direction.

The scheme wasn't foolproof. None were. The men after Lauren might see through the ploy. They could follow the sheriff's department SUV instead of the Jeep provided by the nearest marshal's office. Chris could only hope that blocking traffic for the half hour, as much as it inconvenienced people, would give him enough time to get his charges and himself to safety without the pursuers learning where this time.

They all needed sleep too much to continue as they were. Making mistakes was easy when one was fatigued. Reflexes were slow, reaction time delayed, when seconds counted to save one's life.

Davis's house was as good a haven as they could've hoped for. The fence, effective for keeping deer at bay, wouldn't keep criminals out for long, but long enough to give fair warning. The house itself was solid and warm and possessed amenities like hot water and hot food.

"Help yourself to anything you need." Davis indicated the guest room. "There's a double bed in there if you ladies don't mind sharing, and here are some blankets for the couch for you, Blackwell. There's food in the fridge. I'm off to my aunt's and will come home with piles of Christmas goodies. Call me if you need backup for anything."

He was gone, his truck roaring out of the driveway, leaving his SUV if they needed transportation.

"As if I could interrupt his Christmas dinner with family after all he's done for us already." Chris looked at the exhausted women. "Who wants the facilities first?"

"I'm better off than you two." Donna headed into the kitchen. "I'll see what there is to eat."

Chris turned to Lauren only to find her slumped on the sofa, head lolling.

"Lauren, sweetheart." The endearment slipped out.

He sat beside her. "If you fall asleep like that, you'll get a terrible crick in your neck."

"Mmm." She opened her eyes. "I'm not sure I can move any farther. But I want to wash my hair."

"I like your ponytail." He touched the gathering of glossy strands. "It shows off your beautiful face."

"Chris, don't look at me like that." She pressed her palm against his cheek as though she would turn his face away.

"Like what?"

"Like—like you still care about me for more than your duty."

"I do." He moved just enough to kiss the palm still against his cheek.

She caught her breath. Her lips parted. Her eyes drifted closed. "I've missed you." Her declaration emerged as a mere puff of air brushing his lips.

Then her lips replaced her breath against his mouth. His hand cupped the back of her head, and he was drowning in her sweetness forever.

For the thirty seconds needed for Saber to tear across the great room and wedge herself between them.

Laughing, they broke apart, their gazes meeting, locking.

"That was probably a dumb thing to do," Lauren said.

"Probably." Chris grinned at her dazed expression. "Highly unprofessional of me."

"Shockingly forward of me."

Saber stood between them, wagging from her ears back.

"I—I should get cleaned up while Donna fixes supper. Where's my backpack?" Lauren glanced around.

"Here." Chris picked up the hideous orange bag.

It was heavier than something just carrying clothes and toiletries should be. Through the soft sides, he felt only a small shampoo bottle, the softness of garments—

And something that shouldn't be there.

His guts churning, Chris held the pack with one hand and yanked back the zipper with the other.

"What are you doing?" Lauren demanded.

"What are you doing with this?" Chris pulled his service weapon from Lauren's backpack.

Still reeling from the impact of kissing Chris for the first time in over five years, Lauren stared at the gun without comprehending its significance, nor the implication of Chris's question. That gun did not belong in this moment of sweet remembrance, of admitting she still loved Chris, of knowing their future was no different than it had been five years ago.

"Have you had this the whole time?" Chris asked.

Reality sank in and Lauren flicked her gaze to Chris's face, stiff and pale. She shook her head. "I have no idea what you're talking about. Of course I haven't had it the whole time we've been on the run. Where do you think I hid it when I had nothing but the clothes on my back?"

"I'm trying to figure that out myself. But if you didn't have it, how did it get into your backpack?"

"I have no idea. I remember touching your gun when I was helping you out from under all that wood on my deck, but I have never seen it."

"And it found its way from my deck to your backpack without you ever seeing it or touching it again?" Chris shoved the gun into his waistband at the small of his back. "Lauren, I think you are the smartest person I know, so you understand why I can't believe you."

"I do understand."

All too well.

"I understand that this is why we have no future. You will forever doubt that I am not a criminal in some way myself because I'm loyal to my brother."

She blinked hard. She would not cry in front of him. Not again. She had already made herself too vulnerable when she kissed him. The gesture told him she still cared more than was good for either of them.

The kiss told him he still held the power to break her heart.

"I don't want to think that. I didn't think it. But you have my service weapon in your backpack." Chris's face twisted, his eyes closing.

Suddenly, Lauren realized finding his gun in her bag hurt him as much as his accusation pierced her heart. He wanted her to be innocent, blameless.

He wanted to be free to love her.

"I can't prove I didn't take your gun off my deck. I can't prove the negative." She took a deep breath. "You have to trust I'm telling the truth."

Trust. Not in existence between them.

"But I'm too tired to fight with you." She snatched her bag from his hands and escaped into the guest bedroom. As she closed the door, she heard Donna call, "Supper's ready."

Lauren's stomach knotted at the idea of food. A hot home-cooked meal would be good for her. Being near Chris at that moment would not.

She extracted toiletries from her bag and entered the bathroom. A hot shower and clean hair went a long way to make her feel more capable of handling Chris and his accusations. Sleep would go further. Hair still wet, she crawled into the bed with the sheets smelling of fabric softener, and was asleep in moments.

She thought she would sleep the entire night, provided someone didn't try to kill them and drag her from the only comfortable warmth she had experienced since Ryan came racing across her yard. But she slept for no more than an hour according to her phone. Something had awakened her. A gunshot? A cry for help? Something as normal as Donna dropping the lid of a pan in the kitchen?

Whatever the cause, the house was quiet now. Not silent. Water ran through pipes, and the low murmur of voices occasionally accompanied by music suggested someone watched TV.

Lauren lay motionless, listening for more, breathing deep and slow in the hope she would fall asleep again. She felt better for all the nap had been short, her mind more alert.

Alert and racing too much for sleep.

And that was what had awakened her—her own mind. Maybe she'd dreamed something. Maybe she'd managed to think clearly in her sleep. Whatever the cause, she had an answer.

Reluctant to drag herself into the relatively chilly air of the closed room, she climbed from bed and pulled on her fresh set of clothes with the offhand thought that she should wash her other jeans and T-shirt in the sheriff's washer. Chris would want to wash his things too. Neither of them had many possessions with them.

She had lost so much. If she dwelled on that, sadness threatened to wound her heart. Since losing Chris, possessions were all she had. The most important ones were gone now.

Ryan was out of her life, beyond the pale with his actions in apparently choosing to follow in their father's footsteps. Chris, the most important connection of her life, was beyond even friendship if she couldn't convince him she was telling the truth.

She brushed her hair, now mostly dry, and drew on a touch of lipstick and dab of powder for courage, then exited the bedroom.

Donna sat on the sofa knitting and watching *It's a Wonderful Life* on TV, Saber sprawled on the rug at her feet. Chris sat at the dining table, thumbs flying over the screen of his phone. Sometime in the past hour, he had showered and changed and affixed a fresh bandage to the wound on his scalp. The dog jumped up to greet Lauren with a wagging tail and sloppy grin. Both humans glanced at her before returning their attention to their respective tasks.

"You look more human," Donna said. "There's homemade mac and cheese in the kitchen."

"Sounds good. Thank you." Lauren crossed the living room end of the great room and approached Chris at the table.

He stood, setting his phone on the place mat before him. "How may I help you?"

"The assault on me in the store." She began her idea without preamble. "I don't think they intended to kidnap me or harm me in front of all those people. It's like chasing me out of my house and then burning it, and letting us know they knew we were at the sheriff's office. They are trying to keep us off balance and always moving so we are too tired to be careful."

"I agree with you on that." Chris spoke slowly, as though cautious about agreeing with her.

"And I think there's more to that assault in the store." Lauren's throat was dry. It was so important for Chris to believe her.

"And what is that?" Chris's phone pinged and he looked at it.

She was losing his attention.

"I said they grabbed my backpack and tried to pull it off."

"But you had knotted the straps below the buckles. Yes, I remember." He had picked up his phone and was responding to the latest text.

Rude. Irritating. Dismissive.

Lauren snatched the phone out of his hands and returned it to the place mat with a thud. "Stop that and listen to me. This is important."

"So are text messages from my office."

"Especially ones about me."

She'd read the words on the screen, visible with the response text not yet sent.

"Doing a more thorough background check on me? Looking to see if I've got a speeding ticket?" Her voice throbbed with indignation and sarcasm. "You'll discover I haven't got so much as a parking ticket in the past five years. Not in the past twenty-seven, actually. I never cheated on a test in school or plagiarized someone else's papers in college. Since we broke up, I have gone out on exactly three dates with nice men from my church who bored me to death, and I have paid my taxes without trying to evade a single dollar required of me, even though doing so meant I ate mac and cheese, the generic boxed type, and packaged ramen noodles for weeks in the beginning. But you'll waste resources because my word isn't good enough."

"I found my service weapon in your backpack."

"That's right. You did. Because when that person grabbed it in the store, he wasn't trying to take my backpack. He was putting your gun into it."

Chris's eyes widened. "It's possible. I didn't think—" He broke off. "Have a seat and let me get you some supper."

"I'll get it myself when we've resolved this."

"Please. You look like you need a good meal." He pulled out a chair adjacent to his.

All at once understanding that Chris needed a few minutes to think and the routine of heating up food in a microwave would help the thought process, Lauren acquiesced and sat.

Chris ducked into the kitchen. The refrigerator door opened and closed with a thud. Cabinet doors banged. The microwave hummed. From the far end of the great room, Lauren watched the images on the TV. The movie always made her sad, emphasized her isolation on holidays. Self-imposed isolation for a good reason, but lonely just the same.

She needed to change that, build a network of friends now that she didn't have to devote quite so much time to building her company.

Having a family of friends would help her get over Chris once again.

He exited the kitchen with a plate in one hand and a glass of something that looked like cider or apple juice in the other. The plate he set before her held a square of mac and cheese, oozing with tangy cheese, and a salad. Something healthy and something that was total comfort food.

"It's cider." Chris placed the glass beside her plate. "But I can get you iced tea if you prefer."

"Cider is great." Lauren picked up her fork, hoping eating would calm her knotted stomach.

The first bite of pasta and cheese melted on her tongue with a burst of flavor and creamy goodness. She sighed with pleasure. "Donna, you're a good cook."

"A good thing your dad could afford a cook, since your mother couldn't boil water" came Donna's response.

He'd hired a cook until he went to prison, but her mother left then too.

"You'd think you would be glad you weren't married to him anymore," Chris said.

Donna's needles stopped clacking. "I am."

"Then why do you care so much about Lauren's mother?" Chris asked.

Donna sat in silence for so long Lauren thought she wouldn't respond. Lauren didn't want to eat her salad in the stillness, beyond the lame jingle of a commercial, for fear the crunching lettuce would sound like an army tramping over crusted snow.

Then Donna picked up her needles and resumed knitting what appeared to be the tube of a giant sock. "Nearly thirty years of habit." With that pronouncement, she turned up the volume on the television.

Across the corner of the table between them, Lauren met Chris's eyes and they both laughed. They laughed together with a glance as they had often done in the past.

How can we not be meant to be together? Lauren's heart cried.

"So, do you believe me?" she asked.

"I'm willing to believe it's a distinct possibility." He stretched his hand across the table and touched her fingers as she reached for the glass of cider. "I believe it's a far better solution than the one I leaped to."

"And why did you leap to that conclusion, Chris?"

He looked away. "I think you know."

She did know, and the pasta in her mouth turned to paste. Tasteless and sticky, refusing to go down her throat in anything but a painful lump.

She speared her fork into the salad greens. She should at least eat some more vegetables. "This will end soon, more than likely, and we can go our separate ways again."

"I had hoped we could find our way to being friends," Chris said.

"Friends trust one another." Lauren rose with her plate in hand and stalked into the kitchen.

She found some plastic wrap and covered her plate. Too many lean years had taught her not to waste food. She might be hungry later and want the once-delicious mac and cheese. She might be hungry again when this disastrous Christmas ended.

Oh, Ryan, what were you thinking?

Being in the kitchen as far as she could run away at the moment, though she wished she were anywhere but in northern Michigan on Christmas Eve, Lauren found minor cleaning that needed to be done—a speck of cheese on the counter, putting cleaned cups away, washing the coffee carafe. In the great room, the movie played with some yelling, suggesting the climax. A cell phone rang, and Chris spoke in a voice too quiet for Lauren to catch the words above James Stewart calling out for his wife.

Lauren rubbed the carafe with the dish towel, set it on its hot plate and considered making a pot of coffee. She wanted something hot to drink, and Davis didn't seem to have any tea bags in the house nor hot chocolate.

She reached for the bag of coffee.

"Lauren." Chris stood in the doorway, his phone in hand. "The call is for you."

"On your cell?" Her heart began to pound in a slow, sickening pulse.

"He didn't have your new number." Chris held out his phone. "It's Ryan."

THIRTEEN

Her hand shaking, Lauren took the phone from Chris. "Ryan, where are you? What do you think you're doing, running like this? Why—"

"Be quiet and listen." Though weak and strained, Ryan's voice cut through Lauren's barrage of questions like a shout. "I don't have much time. *We* don't have much time."

"I saw the list. I know about—"

"I need to talk to you." He coughed. "You and Blackwell."

"I'm listening." Lauren managed to control her urge to question or lecture or both. "I can put you on speaker to talk to both of us." She tilted the phone just enough so Chris could bend his head close to hers and listen.

"Not on the phone. I haven't been able to charge mine and the battery is going." He coughed again in a distinct wheeze. "And Blackwell can take me in. Running failed."

Lauren turned her head so she could look into Chris's face. She expected to see triumph, anticipation. She read nothing in his chiseled features. He had schooled them into impassivity.

"How can we find you?" Lauren asked.

"Do you remember our cousin Marcus's fishing cabin?"

"No."

"It's near Grayling, on the Manistee, not the Au Sable."

He gave her directions. She repeated them in the hope that, between the two of them, Chris and she would remember every detail.

"That's nearly fifty miles," Chris said.

"I'll be here." He emitted a sound, half cough, half laugh. "I hope. And, Lauren?"

Chilled by his wheezing coughs, Lauren could barely manage to say, "I'm still here."

"Don't send the law ahead of you. It'll help them find me faster and I need to tell you…things."

He was gone.

Lauren's hand, holding the phone, dropped to her side. She stared at Chris, speechless, hollow as though someone had taken a spoon and scooped out her heart and lungs, leaving her too numb to feel, to breathe.

"You heard all that?" she asked.

"All of it." Chris removed the phone from her nerveless fingers. "I'll go. You stay here."

"He requested me."

"It's a risk. It could be a trap."

"So you think I want to be safe and warm while my brother kills the man I—while he kills you?" Her voice rose. "There's no way I'll do that. There's no way I'll sit here imagining my worst nightmare being fulfilled."

Chris arched one brow. "And what is that?"

"A member of my family killing you."

"Lauren—" He cleared his throat. "I shouldn't take a civilian along."

"Then I'll find a way to get there myself."

Chris studied her face for a moment, then nodded. "I'm afraid you would. No doubt Davis has a snowmobile in his garage and you're determined enough to drive it fifty miles."

Heels clacked in the great room and Donna appeared in the kitchen doorway. Her face was white and stiffer than usual. "Don't hurt my son."

"I'll do my best not to, Donna." Chris spoke to the distraught mother with a gentleness that brought Lauren's heart slamming back into her chest.

She. Must. Not. Love. Him.

But she did.

"How did you know?" Lauren asked.

"He called me and asked if I had Chris's number. Then he hung up before I could just give Chris the phone. A good thing he didn't want your number since you haven't bothered to give me yours."

"I'll give it to you now."

Lauren found a whiteboard hanging beside an old-fashioned landline telephone and wrote down her number. Then she wrote the directions to the cabin where Ryan had holed up.

"Will you be all right here alone?" Chris asked Donna.

"No, but not because I'm afraid of bogeymen coming after me. I'm losing my only son." A single tear rolled down her artificially smooth cheek, then another followed and another. A sob escaped her throat. "My son. If I'd been allowed to raise him, this wouldn't have happened."

Or if Lauren's mother hadn't stolen Richard Delaney from Donna, or a thousand other things beyond their control. If her father hadn't gone to prison and her grandmother hadn't raised Lauren at the lake house, she might have grown up differently as well, been on the wrong side of the law by now, hacking computers instead of saving computers from being hacked.

Compassion for Donna's wounded heart rising within her, Lauren crossed the room to wrap her arms around the older woman. She expected to be rebuffed. Instead, Donna held on, her body shaking with silent weeping for several minutes. Then she pulled away, patted Lauren on the cheek and walked into the powder room, closing and locking the door behind her.

Lauren wiped her own eyes on her sleeve. "We better get going."

Chris nodded. "Bundle up. I'll be back in shortly."

Lauren complied, pulling sweatpants over her jeans, layering a sweater over her T-shirt, then her coat, scarf and boots over two pairs of thin socks. She knew how to dress for the cold. As she pulled her knit cap over her hair and donned gloves, wishing she could afford the lack of dexterity in mittens, which were warmer, she caught sight of a weather report.

"Chris, look." She gestured to the TV.

They would be driving into a snowstorm.

"Lake effect. They always get more snow there than we get here closer to Lake Michigan."

"Can the SUV handle it?"

"It'll have to." He called to Donna, still in the powder room, that they were on their way, then led Lauren into the night.

Beyond the outdoor security lights, the sky was so clear each star shone like heaven's Christmas light display. They should be in church with candles and "Silent Night" and hot chocolate afterward. Not slipping through the darkness to meet her brother before he returned to prison—meeting him because he had given up on running.

And they could be headed into a trap. They could die. She could die without telling Chris she had never stopped loving him.

She would tell him later. Not now, not at the beginning of their journey. In silence, she climbed into the icy SUV. Cold from the vinyl seats seeped through her layered clothing. Her breaths showed like fog, steaming up the windows. A blanket still lay on the back seat. She took it and began to wipe the condensation off the insides of the windows while Chris scraped frost from the outside. Cold air blowing from the heater vents helped the foggy windows. It didn't help her maintain the warmth she had gained inside the house.

Cold poured straight through to her marrow. At that moment, she doubted she would ever find warmth again in her heart.

Over the past five years, she had imagined moments like this. The quarry had been her father, not Ryan. The situation had been the same—her family member, her flesh and blood, caught by the man she had intended to marry. If he felt badly about it, any form of guilt, he would question his suitability for his job. If he didn't feel guilty, he would question his suitability to be her husband. She knew him—had known him.

No, she knew him now. He hadn't changed. He was taking far too long to scrape off the minor layer of frost on the windows. The procrastination said he didn't want to meet her brother face-to-face and take him into custody while she watched.

Because he still loved her?

Fortunately, he climbed into the SUV and sent them shooting out of the driveway before she pursued that line of thought. The instant they hit the main road, he turned on the radio and located a station playing Christmas music. The strains of "O Holy Night" filled the cab of the SUV.

Nothing about what was to happen in an hour or so was going to be holy. But after, maybe as early as tomorrow, she could go to church and thank God that she was still alive. For now, she huddled beneath the blanket and wished the heater would begin to work.

"Doesn't the government extend heaters to their vehicles?" she asked to break the silence between them.

"It's working just fine, Lauren." He turned the vent so it poured hot air onto her face.

"I'm still cold."

"Are you running a fever?" He pulled off his glove and touched the back of his hand to her forehead. "It wouldn't surprise me after what you've been through."

"Maybe."

But she knew she wasn't sick and so did he. She suspected he knew as well as she did her cold stemmed from fear.

"Do you think Ryan would sell us to these men to spare his life and escape?" Chris asked after another quarter hour of celebratory music on the radio and silence between them.

"I don't think so. Ryan has spent too much of his life trying to protect me from anything bad." She sighed. "But he did run from custody and lead those men to my house and to Donna's. Who knows what a man will do to save his own skin when push comes to shove."

Another shiver racked her body.

"You don't need to go, Lauren. I can leave you some-place like a police station and go on my own. It's what I'm supposed to do."

"I told you. I'll just follow somehow."

"Then I think we shouldn't drive in all the way."

She shot him a questioning glance. "What do you mean?"

"Do you still cross-country ski?"

"Of course. But where will we get skis?"

"Davis had a pair of cross-country skis and snow-shoes in his garage."

No wonder he had taken so long to ready the SUV. He hadn't been reluctant to go. He had been loading up equipment to get there with as little commotion as possible.

She most definitely wouldn't tell him she still loved him. If he was this eager to catch her brother, he was thinking of his job, his duty and not of her. Admitting love for him now would simply be too humiliating to bear. She had to protect her heart.

So she didn't accidentally look at him, Lauren kept her gaze on the side window. The view mostly consisted of dark trees and white snow, the occasional flash of a headlight in the side mirror or a house set back from the road, some lit with colorful holiday lights. Watching the passing scenery so closely gave her the first view of snowflakes. Initially, they drifted in lazy spirals like feathers from a pillow shaken too hard. The farther east Chris drove, the heavier the snow became.

"Good old lake-effect snow," Lauren murmured.

Chris cut their speed to a crawl. "This will take us longer. Do you want to call Ryan?"

Lauren picked up Chris's phone and keyed in the

password he gave her. She found the last received number and tapped it, noting Chris had made a phone call after Ryan's. It rang four times, then went to voice mail.

"No answer." She returned the phone to the console. "Did you call backup?"

"I did."

Chris didn't elaborate, and she didn't ask.

Lauren returned to staring out the side window. The snow was so heavy she could barely see the trees along the way. No headlights met them coming from the east and none from behind. They lost their radio station, and Chris found another, distant, staticky.

Then suddenly, headlights blazed into the SUV, glaring off the mirrors, a vehicle twice their size or so it seemed, speeding too fast for the slippery conditions, growing closer... Closer...

Chris spun the wheel, driving them into the opposite lane. The SUV fishtailed, engine roaring. Then the tires caught pavement beneath the layer of snow and they sped east, passing the oncoming traffic with mere inches to spare. Behind them, the truck charged ahead, a black vehicle with oversize tires.

"They're following us." Lauren grasped her knees to hold herself steady.

She would not panic. This was a time for cool heads, for calm.

Beside her, Chris's profile was grim. "Do you think they know where to go?"

"I have no idea. I didn't know my cousin had a fishing cabin out here. I haven't seen him in at least ten years and didn't have much to do with him when I did see him."

"Part of the family business?"

She listened for the edge, the hardness in his tone, but didn't hear it.

She inclined her head. "I expect so. Since I stayed out of the family business, I have no idea who is or is not involved. But you don't have to believe me. It's irrelevant right now."

"It is, but I believe you."

She felt like a starving dog just tossed a slice of stale bread. It was the nicest thing anyone had said to her in too long. Or so she felt, besotted fool that she was.

"Then do you believe me about your gun?"

"I do." He set their speed to a crawl long enough to squeeze her hand. "I'm sorry I doubted you."

Now, that was an entire meal's worth of kindness, a balm for her aching heart for weeks to come.

"Thank you." Her voice was rough. She cleared her throat. "So what do we do now?"

"I think I saw a turnoff up here. Maybe we can go in a back way, especially if those men don't know where we're going exactly."

"We could end up in unplowed territory."

"I think we have to risk it."

So they did. They couldn't stay on the main road with the men in the truck so close.

On the side road, their cell phones lost signal. The radio station turned to static hissing like a taunt. Snow encased their vehicle like a shroud, and ahead the narrow lane ended at a cabin so dark and piled with snow no one could have been there for days. The river ran beyond it, a complete barricade.

"The cabin shouldn't be more than a mile or two from here." Tone full of forced cheerfulness, Lauren rested her hand on the door. "Time to strap on those skis."

Chris donned snowshoes that would have been too large for Lauren. She strapped her feet into the cross-country skis and accepted the flashlight Chris pulled from the back of the SUV. She wouldn't be able to handle it while skiing, but he had another one.

He held up something else, barely visible in the snow-luminous night. "Flares. Ready?"

"I'm ready."

The snow was wet and heavy, making going difficult. She hadn't been on skis yet that year and needed a few minutes to regain her rhythm of gliding steps. Difficult as it was, walking would have been worse.

They followed the line of the river, the gurgle of the water, not yet frozen, guiding them along the way. They didn't talk as they listened for signs of other people in the woods. They turned off the flashlight from time to time to let their eyes adjust to the dark and seek other lights.

They smelled the smoke before they saw or heard anything else. Lauren lifted her head, nostrils flaring at the same time Chris stopped and flicked off the flashlight. "I think we're close. Proceed with caution."

They edged forward, two snow-encrusted figures making no more sound than the wind in the trees and the current of the river. And they reached the cabin—a house, really—with light shining through slits in drapes over a sliding glass door.

Though she stood motionless, Lauren's heart raced ahead of her. If they were right, Ryan was inside. The question was, who else might be there?

"I'm going in," Chris said. "Wait here. If I don't signal you that all's clear, take off and drive for population as fast as you can." Keys jingled, and he handed her the ring. "The SUV keys."

"But he asked for me. I should go in."

"Not with that truck on our tail earlier."

"But, Chris, it's dangerous, isn't it?"

"Which is why I need to go alone. It's my job."

Tell him. Tell him. Tell him.

Now was the time to tell him she loved him, before he stepped into what could be an ambush.

She said nothing. Chris kicked off the snowshoes and headed across the yard. His footfalls made no sound on snow-clad steps and deck. He reached the door and knocked. Lauren held her breath, waiting for a blast of gunfire.

Chris kept out of the direct line of sight to the door or window. He heard nothing from inside the house. From outside, he heard nothing human other than his own breaths and the whisper of his boots through the snow.

He reached the door and knocked. "Ryan, it's Chris Blackwell."

Instinct told him to approach Ryan as a person, not as Deputy US Marshal Chris Blackwell. Doing so might work or might get him killed anyway.

He thought he heard the scrape of chair legs on a wood floor.

"Ryan?"

The door sprang open to the end of a security chain. "Where's Lauren?"

"Around. Are you alone?"

"Are you?"

"For now."

"Bring Lauren up and you can come in." Ryan's voice sounded breathless, weak.

"Let me see if you're alone." Chris would protect Lauren first.

Ryan closed the door. Rattling suggested he was removing the security chain. The door opened again, wide this time, to a living room and dining room combination with a kitchen on the other side of a breakfast bar. Two rooms opened off the great room, both doors open. Men could be hiding behind the doors of those rooms or the breakfast bar, but Chris didn't think so.

"Hurry," Ryan said. "The light will show for miles out here."

Chris turned to call to Lauren, but she was already racing across the yard, slipping and sliding and rushing up the steps to fling herself at her brother.

"You idiot! You shouldn't have run away. Are you sick?"

Ryan extracted himself from her embrace, though he smiled down at her. "I'm sick. I think I have an infection in my leg and maybe pneumonia. I can't keep running." He dropped onto a dining chair, his face white with dark circles like bruises beneath his eyes. "The point of running is done anyway."

Chris closed and locked the door. "What was the point of running, other than making you look guilty before being proved so?"

"They were going to kill me." Ryan rested his elbows on the table and supported his head in his hands. "They're still going to kill me. But I don't have the strength to go on."

"Someone is trying to kill us too. Who is it, Ryan?" Lauren sat beside her brother and rested one hand on his shoulder.

Chris crossed his arms over his chest and leaned against the wall beside the door, loving Lauren for her compassion to her brother despite all he had put her through.

"Why did you drag Lauren into danger, Delaney?" Chris demanded.

"I had to get the thumb drive to someone, and I trusted her to do the right thing with it."

"I turned it over to the Marshals. But it was encrypted."

"It's a hit list," Chris said. "Why is Lauren's name on it?"

"Not that one." Ryan coughed against his sleeve, a dry and harsh seal's bark. "That's nothing. Men who want to eliminate the Delaneys. I got their list, so they want to kill me."

"How did you get it?" Chris felt like he was badgering a sick man, but he needed answers.

"Shouldn't we try to get him out of here first?" Lauren asked. "He needs a doctor."

"Help's on the way," Chris said.

"And the men who want to kill us are too, aren't they?" Ryan said.

"All the more reason why we should leave," Lauren insisted.

"He can't walk out of here." Chris glanced around the room, taking note of a door beyond the kitchen. "Lauren, regardless of who shows up here first, head for that door and get back to the SUV as fast as you can."

"I can't leave—" She stopped herself from protesting and nodded.

Another thing he loved about her—she was so quick to understand a situation. He didn't need to tell her that neither Ryan nor he would benefit from her staying and having her safety as a distraction. If she was out of the way of potential gunfire, Chris could concentrate on staying alive.

"Who are those men?" Chris asked.

"They worked for our father. He fired them for not carrying out his orders as directed. Now they want to kill everyone who knows what they've done."

"I don't know what they've done," Lauren objected. "Why do they want to kill me?"

"Simply because you're Richard Delaney's daughter." Tears spilled down Ryan's face unchecked. "But I had to let her know so she could tell you." He raised his head to look into Chris's eyes. "And then I gave her the USB drive, which made killing her sooner rather than later more important."

"Then why did you do it?" Chris demanded.

"I wanted it to get to you." Ryan was gasping for breath. "That drive holds the proof of who killed your father."

And Ryan possessed it. Ryan, accused of being a henchman for his father.

Chris's knees weakened. He feared he'd be sick as he asked, "Your father?"

Lauren gasped and pressed her hand to her lips, her pupils huge. "No."

"Not directly. But he ordered it."

"Why?" Chris barely managed the single word.

"He learned something from a prisoner and had to be stopped from testifying. Dad didn't want to go back inside and would have. I suspected." Ryan turned to Lauren. "When you broke off things with Blackwell, I wanted to get to the truth. I thought if Blackwell knew, he would leave the Marshals Service and you two could have your life together. But it wasn't that easy. Our own father didn't trust me to be sincere."

"Because you weren't." Relief softened Lauren's features.

"I wasn't. But I pretended I wanted to be part of his dealings to find out and maybe stop him. I wanted above anything to stop him." Ryan wiped his eyes with the backs of his hands and emitted a long, shuddering sigh. "But nothing will stop him except getting locked up again. So I gathered proof and was about to get out when I was arrested on evidence one of Dad's henchmen planted on me. Then the threats came when I was in prison before the trial, and I ran the first chance I got."

"You were going to turn state's evidence," Chris said.

Ryan nodded.

"And they had to kill you before you testified against them."

Ryan nodded again. "And I didn't know who to trust. My father has law enforcement of all sorts on his payroll. So I risked getting the USB drives to you, Lauren, and to Mom. I didn't know they were so close behind. I thought I had time. I thought—"

A thud upon the door warned them none of them had time.

"Lauren, run," Chris shouted.

Then he dived to drag Ryan to the floor as gunfire blasted and the door burst open, its lock blown away. Ryan rolled beneath the table. Chris turned, crouched, fired once, twice.

One man fell back with a cry. Chris shot again—once, twice, three times.

Before a sledgehammer knocked him into the chairs Ryan and Lauren had been sitting on moments earlier.

As blackness overtook him, Chris saw a second man fall.

Lauren raced across the snow. Every instinct of love and protectiveness told her to stay, to somehow help. She did what she had trained herself to do years ago—use her brains. Intelligence said run from gunfire. She was unarmed. She didn't know how to use a gun. She was not bulletproof. She could do nothing but get away so neither man she loved would be distracted by her presence.

If either was still alive. She thought she heard the voices of three men shouting. Two against three weren't terrible odds, but Ryan was so weak and ill, and Lauren hadn't seen a weapon anywhere near Ryan. So it was three against one. Worse odds. If only reinforcements would come.

She would do her best to bring them, show them the way if she could reach the SUV.

She located the skis and slammed her feet into them. She took precious moments to calm herself. She didn't need to fall out there alone in the dark and cold. For the moment, she didn't need to think about what Ryan had said.

She sped along the path they had taken, going faster through the trail she and Chris had cut earlier. It shone in brighter light, and she realized the snow had stopped and moonlight glowed off the white carpet below. A good thing. She couldn't manage a flashlight.

The mile and a half to the SUV felt like it took all night. Gasping—or maybe sobbing—she unlocked the

SUV and tossed the skis into the back. Moments later, she was cranking the engine and roaring out of the narrow road. Somewhere she thought she caught the wail of a siren. Reinforcements. Probably too late.

And she hadn't told Chris she loved him.

Maybe that was good. With the news Ryan had imparted, Chris could never renew their relationship. She was worse than a criminal's daughter. She was the daughter of the man who'd ordered the execution of Chris's father.

Tears blurring her vision, she hit the main road before she saw it. The snow there was packed into icy ruts. The front tires caught and spun, gained traction, sent her jouncing into the far lane. With care, she turned the wheel, trying to steer in the right direction. She hit ice instead and began to spin once, twice.

The back tires slipped into a ditch and held, each attempt at gunning the engine digging the SUV deeper.

And lights blazed in the distance.

Lauren leaped from the SUV and ran toward the trees. Unless the driver of the oncoming vehicle saw the SUV in time, impact was inevitable and she wasn't about to become a human pancake. She plowed through the ditch and took refuge behind a tree.

The oncoming vehicle sat up high. A truck roaring with its speed. Too much speed for the road conditions. He wasn't going to stop soon enough. By the time he spotted the SUV and tried, he was too close. He slammed into the SUV and the truck went airborne.

Lauren ran deeper into the trees. The arc of headlights shone through bare branches. Metal shrieked. Glass shattered. Then silence fell.

Lauren turned back to see the truck roof-down in

the ditch and the sheriff's SUV a mangled heap mere yards away.

By the light of moonlit snow, the truck looked black with oversize tires.

FOURTEEN

Chris didn't remember Christmas Day or the next. Consciousness and memory returned with vague glimpses of uniforms—doctors, nurses, law enforcement of half a dozen different kinds. Civilians arrived in the forms of his mother and sister. Even Donna Delaney stopped to thank him for helping her son, also in the hospital for an infected bullet wound to his leg and double pneumonia.

He was in the hospital under the watchful eye of deputy US marshals.

"He'll have to do some prison time," she said, "but not as much as we feared. He has too much information to share."

"Against his own father?" Chris felt so weak he wasn't sure he spoke loudly enough for her to hear.

"Especially against his own father. Some of that man's employees, as he liked to call them, were helping Ryan all along."

"I knew he had to have accomplices. But he's giving them up for prosecution?"

"Among others."

"And those men after us?"

Donna looked surprised. "Didn't anyone tell you?

You shot two of them and the third one was knocked unconscious when he tried to flee and ran into the SUV Lauren was driving."

"He hit Lauren?" Chris tried to sit up.

Pain drove him back—pain in his heart more than the pain in his chest from his bullet wound.

No wonder she wasn't there. She'd been hurt—or worse.

"Tell me, is she…?" He couldn't say it.

All the things he had thought about Lauren helping her brother stabbed his conscience. All the years they had wasted because he was bent on justice were no more than a waste.

But it wasn't justice he had sought. It was revenge. And revenge was not what the Lord wanted for his life. He had taken into his own hands bringing down the man who'd killed his father and destroyed the best thing he had going for him—Lauren's love.

Now he was too late to realize it and make amends.

"She's all right," Donna said. "When the SUV spun out and went into a ditch, she knew enough to get out and run into the trees before the truck ran into her."

"Smart lady. But why hasn't she come to see me?" He sounded pathetic.

Donna gave him a look of sympathy. "I asked her that myself. She's staying with me, you know, so she can be close to Ryan while he's here in the hospital. But she says she's Richard Delaney's daughter and that will never change."

"That won't, but I can," Chris said.

He had. Being with her again had told him he had his priorities upside down. If only he could talk to her, let her know, ask for forgiveness for not trusting her and ask for another chance.

"You'll have to do some fast talking to convince her," Donna said. "You thought her capable of helping her brother and stealing your gun."

Another thing to beat himself up over—believing she would hide his gun from him.

"I suppose one of the men chasing us stole it and planted it in her backpack."

Donna shook her head. "One of Ryan's accomplices did it to sow discord between you two in the hope you wouldn't work together and compare notes. So you wouldn't find Ryan quickly with Lauren's help."

"It nearly worked."

Because of his need to prove—what? That he was the best deputy US marshal in the division?

"I've made a lot of mistakes," Chris said. "I hope none are irredeemable in her eyes."

"I doubt they are." Donna's touch on his shoulder was kind, nearly maternal.

But not entirely reassuring.

Later that day, when he asked his mother about when he would see Lauren, she merely gave him comforting platitudes. "When you're out of here, we'll see about you visiting her."

But he still hadn't heard from Lauren when he finally got to go home on New Year's Eve.

Sore and weak, he let his mother and sister pamper him, pushing an ottoman beside the sofa for his feet, building the fire in the fireplace, giving him an endless supply of hot chocolate and Christmas cookies. In the corner, the tree still shone in multicolored glory, wrapped presents beneath. His family had waited for him to celebrate. They would open gifts on New Year's Day.

He bit off another point of a cookie shaped like a star and savored the buttery sweetness on his tongue. This was what he had so wanted when he'd set out from Chicago over a week ago. As much as he loved being with his mom and sister, his life didn't hold the same completeness he thought it would once he knew who had killed his father. Now the career decision he had made seemed pointless like the star cookie in his hand. It was just a circle with no clear direction.

He set the sweet aside, no longer hungering for his mother's superb baking. He closed his eyes and recalled the most delicious meal he'd eaten of late—the bacon, lettuce and tomato sandwich Lauren had prepared for him. Simple fare from a delightfully complex lady.

"I like the tree-shaped ones myself." At the sound of the voice, Chris's eyes flew open.

"Lauren?"

She stood in the center of the room, gazing at him, her lips curved in a tentative smile. "Hi, Chris. I hope you don't mind. Donna said you wanted to see me."

"I've wanted to see you since I regained consciousness. Where were you?"

"I've been here for an hour and a half, talking to your mom and trying to get up the courage to come in to see you." She bowed her head. "I've been giving you time to adjust to the idea you almost married the daughter of the man who had your father killed."

"I almost married the lady I love." He held out his hand. "The lady I still love. The lady I still want to marry."

"Chris, you can't. I'm still Richard Delaney's daughter. You're still a deputy US marshal. I don't think the two facts mix well."

"Neither do I."

Something flashed in Lauren's golden-brown eyes. "Then why did you want me to come all this way to see you?"

"To tell you—will you sit? I'm getting a crick in my neck."

She hesitated, then sat beside him on the sofa. "What did you want to say that Donna claims needed to be said in person?"

Chris faced her, one hand covering hers where it rested on the cushions. "I was wrong. I joined the Marshals Service for all the wrong reasons. They were reasons so wrong I couldn't see what was right and good in my life. That's you. I love you and want a second chance, or at least a chance to show you your father's and brother's activities have nothing to do with you."

"They may to your bosses."

"Then I need different bosses." He touched his chest. "This is probably going to render me unfit for anything but desk duty anyway, and I'd die of boredom with that."

Lauren's eyes widened. "Will you go back to the law?"

"In some capacity. Maybe prosecuting attorney. I don't know yet. I have time to decide." He caressed her fingers. "You can have time to decide too. As much as you like, but I hope it's not a lot. We've wasted too much already."

She peeked at him through her lashes. "What am I supposed to be deciding?"

"If you can love me again."

"I never stopped. When I was running away from

that cabin, I kept thinking how you could be killed and I never told you I still love you."

"Will you tell me now?"

"I love you, Chris. A thousand times over to make up for all the times I just couldn't. My dad. Your dad. My brother getting you shot. Are you certain?"

"More than anything. More than I was five years ago." Though pain twinged through his ribs, he turned so he could grasp her other hand. "Will you marry me, Lauren Wexler Delaney?"

"As soon as we can." She leaned toward him.

He bent his head and their lips met as the clock struck midnight. A new year for a new beginning in their life together.

* * * * *

If you enjoyed this book, pick up these other exciting Christmas stories from Love Inspired Suspense:

Military K-9 Unit Christmas
by Valerie Hansen and Laura Scott
Holiday Amnesia
by Lynette Eason
Lone Star Christmas Witness
by Margaret Daley
Bodyguard for Christmas
by Carol J. Post
Cold Case Christmas
by Jessica R. Patch

Find more great reads at www.LoveInspired.com.

Dear Reader,

Thank you for taking a chance on me, an author new to contemporary romantic suspense. Romance and suspense are an irresistible combination and I am thrilled to share Chris and Lauren's story.

Besides the danger in which Chris and Lauren find themselves, this is a story about a second chance at love. In the past, they allowed self-doubt, shame and anger to get in the way of the life God intended them to share. Now they have a second opportunity, not just at that love but at making their hearts right with God, setting their priorities straight and looking forward instead of into a past they cannot change.

As for the setting, I couldn't resist a Michigan winter. It's a place and season I happen to adore.

I love to hear from my readers. You can contact me through my website, www.lauriealiceeakes.com, or find me on Twitter, @laurieaeakes, or on Facebook as Author Laurie Alice Eakes.

Warmly,
Laurie Alice Eakes

SPECIAL EXCERPT FROM

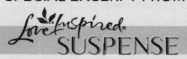

Love Inspired.
SUSPENSE

*With a price on his witness's head,
US marshal Jonathan Mast can think of only
one place to hide Celeste Alexander—in the
Amish community he left behind. But will this trip
home save their lives…and convince them that a
Plain life together is worth fighting for?*

Read on for a sneak preview of
Amish Hideout *by Maggie K. Black,
the exciting beginning to the Amish Witness Protection
miniseries, available January 2019
from Love Inspired Suspense!*

Time was running out for Celeste Alexander. Her fingers flew over the keyboard, knowing each keystroke could be her last before US marshal Jonathan Mast arrived to escort her to her new life in the witness protection program.

"You gave her a laptop?" US marshal Stacy Preston demanded. "Please tell me you didn't let her go online."

"Of course not! She had a basic tablet, with the internet capability disabled." US marshal Karl Adams shot back even before Stacy had finished her sentence.

The battery died. She groaned. Well, that was that.

"You guys mind if I go upstairs and get my charging cable?"

The room went black. Then she heard the distant sound of gunfire erupting outside.

"Get Celeste away from the windows!" Karl shouted. "I'll cover the front."

What was happening? She felt Stacy's strong hand on her arm pulling her out of her chair.

"Come on!" Stacy shouted. "We have to hurry—"

Her voice was swallowed up in the sound of an explosion, expanding and roaring around them, shattering the windows, tossing Celeste backward and engulfing the living room in smoke. Celeste hit the floor, rolled and hit a door frame. She crawled through it, trying to get away from the smoke billowing behind her.

Suddenly a strong hand grabbed her out of the darkness, taking her by the arm and pulling her up to her feet so sharply she stumbled backward into a small room. The door closed behind them. She opened her mouth to scream, but a second hand clamped over her mouth. A flashlight flickered on and she looked up through the smoky haze, past worn blue jeans and a leather jacket, to see the strong lines of a firm jaw trimmed with a black beard, a straight nose and serious eyes staring into hers.

"Celeste Alexander?" He flashed a badge. "I'm Marshal Jonathan Mast. Stay close. I'll keep you safe."

Don't miss
Amish Hideout *by Maggie K. Black,*
available January 2019 wherever
Love Inspired® Suspense books and ebooks are sold.

www.LoveInspired.com